Tropical Depression

A Novel Written by Larry Dickens

I hope you enjoy it, Mary!

Larry

This book is a work of fiction. Places, events, and situations in this story are purely fictional. Any resemblance to actual persons, living or dead, is coincidental.

ISBN: 1-4033-4825-1 (e-book)
ISBN: 1-4033-4826-X (Paperback)

This book is printed on acid free paper.

1st Books - rev. 09/13/02

Cover Credits

Cover design by Elaine Gotham, Gotham City Design, 585-374-9585

Cover satellite imagery courtesy of NOAA (see Acknowledgments page for entire credit)

Back cover photograph of Larry Dickens © 1998 Larry Dickens

Trade Routes of the
SS *Majestic Prince*

For John and Jane Prislopski
One could find no finer mother-and-father-in-law

Chapter One

Specks of Light

At first, one could see them appear as nothing more than distant specks of light.

Looking down at the ocean through the clear, night sky from a position miles above the earth, they appeared tiny against an awesomely huge, black background. In the vastness of this body of water, they were the *only* sparkles of light to be seen for hundreds of square miles. Alone and insignificant. Miniscule and defenseless. Points of light which, had they been suddenly extinguished by some unknown force in the immense black sea, would not have been missed.

However, descending through the night sky, one would begin to see these points of light grow in size, and then split, separate, and become two distinguishable lights. Continuing even closer, one could identify two other lights - one red, the other green. One would suddenly recognize that the tiny, insignificant specks of light were actually the navigation lights of two vessels, floating on the surface of the water, silently passing through it. They seemed suspended, hovering between the infinite sky and stars above and the murky, unseen, ocean floor four miles below. Two ships in the middle of the South China Sea, en route to somewhere.

The navigation lights of any ship represented something far greater than the insignificant and miniscule. Behind the solitude of these lights there were human beings onboard. The larger of the two, the Japanese supertanker *SS Nagoya Wan*, had a crew of twenty-four;

1

the other, the Filipino ferry *M/V Batan,* carried a crew of twelve and four hundred passengers. Both carried men and women, each with their own lives, their own dreams, hopes, ambitions, desires, and feelings. The fact they were the *only* human beings for thousands of square miles on the surface of this deserted, watery plane was not a concern to these seafaring people. For the crewmembers it was part of the turf inherited with life at sea.

The ships' navigation lights burned brightly. The smaller ferry was on the supertanker's starboard side and crossing. The two vessels were closing and on a dangerous collision course.

■ ■ ■

Manning the bridge of the nine hundred feet long, Japanese supertanker stood the captain with his third officer and helmsman. The third officer was nervous, and with good reason.

"Captain, he has the right of way," the twenty-eight year-old junior third officer spoke, offering a reminder to the man who was his well-seasoned superior. "Shouldn't we change course for him?"

The captain ignored his comment for a moment. Instead, he looked at the helmsman. "Helmsman, hold your course."

"Aye, sir," the seaman replied as he made small adjustments to his wheel.

The captain then turned to the third officer and addressed his concerns. "He'll go around us. These local ferries are a hell of a lot more maneuverable than we are."

At fifty-five, the captain had been through situations like this more times than he could remember. "Besides, we're bigger than he is," he added, in a lame attempt to inject some humor into the situation.

The third officer was not amused by the captain's disregard for the International Rules of the Road that dictated that a vessel crossing from starboard to port was to be avoided. He noted no change in the ferry's bearing. "But we're getting close, sir. He's less than a half-mile away."

The captain dismissed the man's concerns. "Don't worry so much. These ferries always wait until the last second and then they turn. Relax."

The third officer, however, was unable to relax. Despite the fact the captain had assumed the conn - i.e., command of the bridge - thus removing the responsibility of the traffic situation from his shoulders, he still felt nervous. The knot in his stomach tightened.

■ ■ ■

Nine hundred feet away, on the bow of the supertanker, the seaman on lookout duty was watching the Filipino ferryboat, also with increasing concern. He picked up the bow telephone and called the bridge.

When the third officer answered the phone, the seaman reported, "Bridge, this is the bow. This ferry is getting real close."

Before the third officer could relay the lookout's message to the captain, the captain suddenly ordered, "Blow the danger signal." It was clear that the skipper was now worried.

The third officer dropped the telephone and rushed to the ship's whistle button. He pressed it repeatedly. The huge, forward mast whistle bellowed out tremendous, deafening blasts into the night air. The bow lookout grimaced and, dropping his telephone to the deck, instantly clutched his ears to protect his hearing.

The whistle blew five blasts - the international danger signal.

■ ■ ■

The ferryboat *M/V Batan* was en route from Manila to Kao-hsiung. The third officer on the bridge watched with apprehension as the huge supertanker approached on his port side. He assumed, however, that the ship was going to turn and pass astern of it, as was required by the International Rules of the Road. By those same rules he was obligated to hold his course, unless collision was unavoidable. In that case, a departure from the Rules was allowed.

The *Batan* was filled to capacity that night, with four hundred passengers onboard. At that late hour most of the passengers were deep in sleep. Most were returning home from a weekend in the Philippines. None had any idea of the situation developing on either vessel's bridge.

As the supertanker blew the danger signal, the third officer knew it was far too late. Both ships were now too close for any collision avoidance maneuver to be effective. Any departure from the Rules would not make a bit of difference.

■ ■ ■

The supertanker broadsided the ferry on her port side; tore it open like a soda can and ripped it in two. As the *Nagoya Wan* plowed through it, the tanker's bow lookout grabbed the phone and shouted to the bridge above the noise of the grinding steel, "God, we've hit her!" No sooner had he spoken when he heard the screams of passengers as the stricken vessel passed down both sides of the *Wan*.

At exactly the same time, the *Nagoya Wan's* captain shouted, "Full astern!"

Both sections of the ferry quickly rolled over and lay on their sides. Both sections instantly went dark and then began sinking as the tanker passed through it and left it in its wake. One by one, life jacket lights began to dot the ocean surface.

The Japanese captain ran outside onto the supertanker's bridge wing just as both halves of the ferry cleared the stern of his ship. He could barely see them in the loom of the *Nagoya Wan's* stern light. Huge, darkened hulks bobbed listlessly in the black waters. As he ran outside onto the bridge wing, he shouted, "Hard left! Full ahead!" to his helmsman and mate. His plan was to circle around and rescue. Looking at the dots of light quickly multiplying on the surface, the captain was overwhelmed by the number of people in the water. His mouth trembled. No words came out. He recognized with agony the magnitude of the disaster he had just created.

In a state of near panic, the captain raced back into the wheelhouse and shouted to his mate, "There's too many of them. Call the radio officer immediately. Tell him to send a distress message! Tell him to call for help!"

Specks of light were everywhere.

Chapter Two

James Briscoe

From high above the vast, darkened body of water that was the South China Sea, another speck was visible. The *SS Majestic Prince*, a liquefied natural gas carrier, was traveling southbound to Sumatra. Owned and operated by GascoTrans, the American flag vessel specialized in transporting liquefied natural gas from the gas fields and jungle ports of Indonesia to the power-starved, utility companies of Japan. The *Prince* had been traversing the South China Sea for over twenty years in the "LNG trade" as it was called. An enormous ship, nine hundred and thirty-six feet long, it's deadweight was in excess of one hundred thousand tons and it had a draft of thirty-six feet. Its navigation bridge sat twelve stories above the waterline. One of the largest tankers of its kind in the world, the *Majestic Prince* was en route from Japan to Sumatra.

It was shortly after midnight when the auto alarm bell went off in the radio room and a message began to hammer out on the old, dot-matrix printer. In the adjacent stateroom, the sharp ringing jolted radio officer Sam Waerhauser out of a sound sleep. He groggily rolled out of bed and then stumbled into the radio room where he clicked on the overhead light. A short, stout man of sixty-three, with a mane of thick white hair, he rubbed the sleep from his eyes as the printer continued to print. When it stopped, he tore off the message and read it. Sam's eyes widened as the urgency of the message registered in his mind and he then quickly carried it down the passageway to the captain's room where he banged on the door.

Several seconds later, Tyler Leech answered the door. The *Prince's* captain towered over the radio operator. His six-foot, two-inch frame filled the doorway.

"What is it?" the sixty-six year-old master muttered, his voice stern and deep. He was half-asleep.

"This just came in, Captain," Sam said with urgency, looking up at the weather-beaten face of the "Old Man."

Captain Leech took the message and read it. He immediately reached for his telephone and called the bridge.

To the mate on watch, he said, "Copy this position down." He then read the latitude/longitude coordinates to the mate on watch. "Figure out how far we are from it. I'll be right up."

■ ■ ■

The *Nagoya Wan* had circled around and stopped in the middle of the disaster of its own making. The bisected ferryboat *Batan* had totally slipped below the ocean's surface. All that remained were life jacket lights seemingly everywhere. The Japanese crew rallied and was busy helping the ferry victims aboard using the tanker's gangways.

On the bridge the third officer announced, "Captain, an American LNG ship has answered our distress. They're only ninety miles away and will be here by 0500."

The distraught Japanese captain wiped the cold sweat from his forehead. "Very well," was all he could say.

■ ■ ■

The *SS Majestic Prince* turned from its course, leaving a tight, circular wake. The tightness of the turn, in addition to her twenty-knot operating speed, caused the huge ship to shudder. This effect, reminiscent of a minor earthquake, was a typical characteristic of the ship's one hundred thousand ton mass fighting to be pointed in a new direction.

The shuddering vibration woke Chief Mate James Briscoe. He lay there in his bed half-expecting the telephone to ring. Ships generally travel in straight lines, going from waypoint to waypoint. Sharp, dramatic turns in the middle of the night in the middle of the South China Sea were not the norm. A sharp turn was done either for a traffic situation or for answering a distress call. A distress call would mean his telephone would ring. As second in command of the *Prince*, it was his job to organize the crew for rescue operations.

Traffic situation or distress. Which is it? he asked himself as he lay there wondering.

No sooner had he finished this thought, the wall phone next to his bed rang and shattered the silence.

Reaching into the dark, he found and lifted the handset off the phone and answered, "Chief Mate. What's happening?"

Briscoe was thirty-five years old and an athletic, six-footer in prime physical condition. A magna cum laude alumnus of the prestigious Massachusetts Maritime Academy located in Buzzards Bay, he was a widely respected chief mate throughout the GascoTrans fleet. He was considered a fair and considerate man, knowledgeable and resourceful.

The "Old Man" was on the other end of the phone.

"Mr. Bris-coe. We have a rescue situation. Prepare the deck. Gangways, lifeboats, the works."

Hearing the word "rescue" was quicker than a jolt of coffee to wake a man from a dead sleep. Briscoe's blue eyes, usually warm, now turned focused and serious.

"Yes, sir. On my way," he assured Leech, and then bolted out of bed.

■ ■ ■

It was morning twilight and the stars were still visible when the *Majestic Prince* arrived on the scene. Second mate Mike Heyerdahl spotted the *Nagoya Wan* through his binoculars. As the *Prince* approached the disaster scene he was astounded.

"Look at all of the people floating in the water around that tanker," Heyerdahl said in disbelief. "There must be hundreds!"

Leech looked through his own binoculars and nodded, acknowledging the sight. "We'll drift in parallel to the tanker," Leech said, and then ordered, "Stop engines!"

7

"Stop engines!" Heyerdahl repeated as he pushed the engine control throttle to the stop position. Several seconds later the *Majestic Prince's* forty-eight thousand horsepower steam turbine engines came to a stop and waited for its next command.

■ ■ ■

Briscoe was on deck directing operations. He had the deck gang prepare the ship's two lifeboats for launching. Lowered to the water's edge, both were manned and ready to go, if needed. The lifeboats could also be used like elevators to retrieve and hoist entire groups of passengers aboard without ever being released from their falls. He also had the deck gang lower both the port and starboard gangways to the water where crewmembers were stationed to help survivors aboard.

Briscoe was working with Bosun Billy Knuckles. A reliable, crusty old-timer, Knuckles was Briscoe's right-hand man in the deck department.

"Bosun, get a couple of cargo nets out here to give these people something to grab on to. Hang them off both sides by the gangways."

"Will do," the Bosun said, and sent two of the sailors to fetch them.

■ ■ ■

The *Majestic Prince* drifted gently into the large group of human beings in the water. Tired and cold, the Filipinos had been in the water for more than four hours. Fearful survivors began grabbing and clutching at the cargo nets and climbed their way up to the inclined gangway. Due to the *Prince's* high freeboard, the main deck was forty-feet above the waterline, thus resulting in a gangway that was over fifty-feet long. The *Prince's* crewmembers assisted the survivors onto the gangway. Before long, too many panicked survivors pushed and shoved their way up the net and crossed over to the gangway. People climbing over other people to reach a safe haven; the innate desire to live driving people to abandon care for their fellow survivors. Despite the confusion, Bosun Knuckles was the first to see it. Standing by the gangway's winch control, he looked up and noticed one of the strands on the gangway hoist wire had parted and was unraveling.

Knuckles hollered down to the men assisting at the bottom of the gangway. "The hoist wire is going to part! Keep those people off! Don't let any more on!" Calling out to Briscoe, he yelled, "Chief Mate! Problem on the starboard gangway!"

Briscoe turned to look just as the gangway hoist wire parted altogether with a dull and resounding snap. The gangway support bridle dropped instantly. Everyone on the gangway screamed as it plummeted. Crewmember Mo Silalahi, who had been helping the survivors onto the lower gangway platform, was hit on the head by the falling steel bridle and knocked down onto the gangway treads. The gangway itself dropped four feet before it was caught by the synthetic backup line and bridle that stopped it instantly. The gangway bounced several times, as if it were suspended at the end of a bungee cord.

"Silalahi's been injured," the bosun yelled to Briscoe.

While survivors on the gangway fell down and clung to the steps, survivors near the end of the gangway lost their balance and fell back into the water. One aging survivor who was already in the water was hit by one of the falling people and knocked nearly unconscious. Along with many others, he was not wearing a life jacket.

Racing to the top of the gangway, Briscoe looked down and saw Silalahi lying at the other end of the gangway where he had been struck, rivulets of blood streaming down the seaman's forehead. He shouted to Cargo Engineer Brad Bensinger who was assisting survivors on deck, "Brad, help me get Silalahi on deck. Hurry!"

The gangway finally stopped bouncing. Survivors still on the gangway began crawling their way up the remaining distance to the main deck. Briscoe and Bensinger rushed down it, pushing past the upward moving flow of frightened people and to the lower platform where seaman Silalahi was injured. Arriving at their shipmate, they lifted him up by his arms, and helped him up the gangway. He was groggy, but able to walk with assistance.

Just as they reached the top of the gangway, Briscoe glanced down at the water forty-feet below and saw the old man in the water without a life jacket. The man looked like he was about to pass out.

Briscoe shouted to the other survivors in the water. "Hey! There! That man! Somebody help him!"

None of the survivors in the water understood English, nor did anyone see that the old man was in danger.

Briscoe repeated, "Hey! Somebody *help* that man! Hey!"

Releasing Silalahi, Briscoe quickly removed the two-way radio from his belt and handed it to engineer Bensinger. "Hold this." To Bosun Knuckles and his men on deck, he hollered, "Throw me a line!"

Realizing what Briscoe was about to do, Bensinger warned, "No, Jimmy, don't do it!"

Too late. Briscoe rushed down the gangway, leaving Bensinger with Silalahi, and pushed his way through the survivors. Reaching the crippled gangway's end, he saw the old man going under. Briscoe dove off the end of the gangway platform and began swimming for him. On deck, many of the *Prince's* crewmembers watched in disbelief.

Captain Leech, watching the rescue operation from the bridge wing, was dumbfounded. "What the devil? What's my chief officer doing in the water?"

Briscoe propelled himself underwater and, a few moments later, resurfaced with the old man under his arm. The old man was still breathing. Just then a life ring with a line attached splashed two feet in front of them. He looked up to the main deck and saw Bosun Knuckles at the other end of the line. With the old man under his arm, Briscoe swam for the ring.

As the wind whipped sea spray in his face, Briscoe said to the fading old man, "Come on, old-timer. You're going to make it. You're going to make it! Hang in there!"

At that moment the old man regained consciousness and smiled gratefully at Briscoe as the two men reached the life ring. Applause erupted from the *Majestic Prince's* euphoric crew and could be heard all the way down to the water's surface.

A month later, there was even more applause.

Chapter Three

Hero and Ruins

It was graduation day at the Massachusetts Maritime Academy and the entire class was applauding. The late spring weather was perfect: sunny, blue sky, puffy, cumulous clouds lazily drifting by. Massachusetts Maritime, the nation's oldest maritime academy, was located on the Buzzards Bay side of the Cape Cod Canal. Dressed in their sterling, Navy dress white uniforms, the cadets and faculty looked splendid. The class and visitors were seated outdoors in the parade field in the center of the campus. The campus sat on a peninsula, surrounded on two sides by water and on one side by the canal. The Academy's training ship sat quietly in the background, as though she were proudly overseeing the annual event. The one hundred graduating cadets had spent countless hours studying and working within her steel bulkheads and upon her steel decks to become deck and engine officers. They were now leaving the nest and the training ship would never see them again.

The applause subsided.

Academy President Admiral Harrington stood at the podium and addressed the class and visitors.

"For courage and bravery beyond the normal call of duty, for the finest display of professionalism under extraordinary circumstances which resulted in the saving of dozens of lives, the Massachusetts Maritime Academy is proud to present this year's Seamanship Award to our guest speaker, Academy-graduate, class of 1987, Mr. James Briscoe."

Larry Dickens

Another large round of applause erupted from the audience as Briscoe stood and made his way to the podium. His wife Heather and their two children, Gilly and Katey, watched proudly in the audience.

Gilly Briscoe shouted out, "Go, Dad, go!"

Briscoe smiled at both his children and stepped up to the podium.

President Harrington enthusiastically shook Briscoe's hand and handed him the award.

"Good, job, Jimmy," President Harrington said.

"Thank you, President Harrington." Turning to the audience, the applause finally died down and Briscoe spoke. "President Harrington, Board of Trustees, Academy Faculty, friends and families, and the Class of 2000: Thank you for honoring me with this most prestigious award. I must say this is not the type of award one actually seeks to acquire during one's career, only because it means that you have to go through something completely unpredictable, horrendous, and extraordinary. Most of us who work on the sea would just as soon have quiet, smooth, and boring voyages, with no heroics. Nature, however, is both our friend and foe out there, and is not always so cooperative. When she isn't, we have to draw from ourselves and our training to reign over the day. It wasn't that long ago that I was sitting there amongst you, my visor cap in hand, ready to fling to the sky, and leap onto whatever ship would have me. Back then it was easy to find a ship. Seagoing American jobs were plentiful. Today it's a dramatically different world. A world full of shipping companies flying flags of countries we've never heard of before. "Flags of Convenience" they are called; where a ship owner can go and save a buck by operating under sub-standard safety requirements using poorly trained crews. Sadly, the United States, the most powerful country, both economically and militarily, in the world has allowed its merchant marine to deteriorate to the point of near extinction. Few of you - you who have spent four, hard years preparing for this day - will ever find seagoing employment under the American flag. For those lucky few of you who do find it, rest assured that your training here at this Academy has prepared you for whatever nature and fate decides to throw at you. My presence here today is proof of that. If it hadn't been for the training I received while I was a cadet at this institution, the outcome of the *M/V Batan* ferry rescue may have been tragically different. Thank you all very much, and the best of luck to all of you."

Applause erupted again.

■ ■ ■

Early December came and a heavy, afternoon blizzard was raging at the Briscoe home in Vermont. The white colonial looked warm and welcoming, its windows brimming with Christmas lights. Three feet of snow had already fallen on the ground.

In the family room, Heather Briscoe stood alone by the window watching the snow fall on their steep driveway. Jimmy had just finished shoveling it and was taking off his coat by the entranceway closet. A lean, fit woman with soft features, dark brown eyes, and long, brown hair, she and Jimmy had met through mutual friends during one of his vacation periods from sea. She was a hometown girl who had a successful graphic design business. For both of them, it had been love at first sight.

Across the room behind her, the logs in the fireplace burned brightly while the kids played a video game on the family television. Otto, their happy, Old English sheepdog, lounged in front of the fire enjoying the radiating warmth and watching the kids play. His cheeks flushed from the cold, Briscoe entered the room and saw her standing there.

Heather was pensive. She said, "The Farmer's Almanac predicts the winter will be a bad one. I hope we don't have any trouble getting up the driveway."

Jimmy Briscoe walked up behind his pretty wife, wrapped his arms around her waist, and held her tight. He pressed his lips to her brown hair and gently blew through its strands, while looking out the window at the snow.

"No problem, honey," he said. "We'll just get a good running start in front of the garage and shoot up the hill. Momentum will carry us the rest of the way." Turning to his children, he said, "Come on kids! Let's go get our Christmas tree."

Katey, three years-old, and Gilly, four, dropped their video game joysticks and responded in unison, "Yea, Daddy!!"

Gilly led Katey by the hand to the entranceway closet and they pulled out their snow clothes.

Briscoe turned Heather around and pulled her close. "Come on, 'Captain of the house,'" he said warmly. "This is an 'all hands' call out."

13

Heather smiled and kissed him. "Okay, Chief Mate."

■ ■ ■

Briscoe led Heather and the children out into the winter wonderland of fresh snow. As he shoveled the driveway again, the entire family became sidetracked into a frolicking snowball fight. Otto barked at them through the window. Briscoe and Heather felt like kids again.

"It'll be dark soon," Heather noted.

Briscoe said, looking skyward, "Yes, we'd better go and get the tree. Everybody in the car."

Gilly asked, "Where are we going to get the tree?"

Briscoe answered, "To Bennett's."

"They've got good trees there," the little boy said.

They climbed into the family car and Briscoe started the engine. On the first attempt up the steep driveway, the Volvo's wheels spun out. Briscoe let the white car roll back down the hill until it was in front of the garage. He then punched the accelerator, the vehicle gained momentum, and the car cruised effortlessly up the hill and out onto the road.

The kids gleefully cheered their father's successful effort.

■ ■ ■

Arriving at Bennett's Christmas Tree Farm, they turned onto the snow-covered, gravel driveway beside the familiar "Cut Down Your Own Tree" sign and parked the car. While Briscoe took the band saw out of the trunk, Gilly and Katey jumped out of the car and ran excitedly around the acres of trees in search of the perfect Christmas tree. After awhile, it was Katey who called out.

"This one, Daddy!"

Gilly agreed. "Yeah! That's our tree!"

Heather and Briscoe surveyed the chosen tree. It was huge; a blue spruce, nearly six-feet tall and perfectly shaped.

"It's beautiful, kids," Heather said warmly. "It has Christmas written all over it and will look perfect in the living room."

"It sure will," Briscoe said. "All right then. *This* is the one."

Stepping up to the tree, he sawed the trunk as close to the ground as he could, and cutting through the last bit of tree trunk, Briscoe shouted, "Timber!"

The kids backed out of the way as the tree toppled over. The children "oohed" and "aahed" when it hit the ground. Heather laughed and snapped photographs of the occasion.

■ ■ ■

Darkness had arrived by the time they returned home. Briscoe brought the tree in through the front door and Heather directed the set-up operation in the living room. The family of four decorated the tree with colored, miniature lights, tree ornaments, and tinsel. Upon finishing, all agreed that it was absolutely beautiful.

With the kids tucked in bed, Briscoe and Heather lay on the couch in front of the glowing fireplace, holding each other as they watched the tree's colorful lights twinkle.

"It was a fun day, Jimmy," Heather said with a smile. "The kids had a ball."

"Yes, they did."

"I wish it could always be like that. I wish you were home for all of our Christmases."

Briscoe nodded, "Me, too, honey. Someday...after retirement."

He gave her a loving hug and stroked her hair as they admired the tree.

"I can't wait to play Santa Claus," he said.

"I can't wait to watch. You haven't been our Santa in two years," she observed.

Just then the telephone rang in the kitchen. Apprehension swept Heather's face. They weren't expecting any calls. She rose and went to answer it.

"Hello?" she asked. "Just a moment, please." She covered the mouthpiece and said, "Jimmy, it's for you. It's your boss, Mr. Franklyn."

"That's odd. He rarely calls during the vacation."

Heather frowned. "He rarely calls at all. I hope it's not that master's job you've been waiting for. At Christmas time?"

Briscoe looked at Heather and shrugged as he took the phone.

"Hello, Mr. Franklyn."

Mr. Franklyn said, "Jimmy, I'm sorry to disturb you and your family during your holiday vacation, but I'm afraid I have some bad news. I'm sure you're aware that Barney Hubbard and his wife, Marilee, were expecting a baby toward the end of January."

"Yes, of course," Briscoe replied.

"Well, the baby arrived early and Marilee had an extremely difficult time with the delivery. The baby didn't make it and they're not sure if she will."

"Oh God," Briscoe said gravely and closed his eyes for a moment.

Her husband's serious tone told Heather the story and she suddenly felt her holiday spirits drain away.

Franklyn continued. "Naturally, Barney needs to come home as soon as possible. I'm afraid you're the only chief mate I have available on my roster that I can send to Japan to relieve him."

"Sure," Briscoe said with disappointment. Glancing helplessly at Heather, he added, "I'd be glad to help."

Heather rolled her eyes. She adamantly yet silently mouthed, "No! You missed the last *two* Christmases!" She threw down her arms, shook her head in frustration, and left the room.

Briscoe felt helpless. He was torn between his own family's needs and that of his friend's.

Franklyn said, "Thanks, Jimmy. I'm sorry to have to disrupt your holiday plans. I know you haven't been home for Christmas in a few years. I'll try to make it up to you. We still have you in mind for that master's job."

Blandly, Briscoe said, "Thanks, Mr. Franklyn," and hung up the phone.

■ ■ ■

Two days later a snowplow drove by the Briscoe home leaving a two-foot ridge of snow at the top of the driveway. The sound of the plow woke Katey and, peeking out of her bedroom window, she was dazzled by the amount of fresh white stuff that had fallen during the night. Just then, she heard her bedroom door creak open, as Gilly poked his head inside.

"Gilly, look at the snow!" she whispered.

Gilly wasn't interested. "Snow, shmow. Katey, come downstairs and see what I found!"

Both children crept silently down the stairs and into the living room.

"Wow! Look at the toys!" Katey exclaimed. Toys had mysteriously appeared overnight and surrounded the new Christmas tree.

"Shh!" Gilly said. "Santa's been here!"

Katey said, "But it's not Christmas yet!"

Both children scurried around the tall tree. Their eyes were wide and bright as they discovered the secrets around it. Hanging on the fireplace were stockings overflowing with candy, and an electric train set looped around the tree, waiting for Gilly to flip the switch. Katey found a lovely Madame Alexander doll that stood nearly as tall as she. New children's books were propped up against colorfully wrapped presents: *Harry Potter and the Goblet of Fire,* and *Mrs. McGillacuddy's Garden Party.* Razor scooters stood by, waiting for their proud, new owners to take them for a spin. A new Christmas dress hung in the corner beside the tree, awaiting Katey. Gilly found the switch and the model train began running around the track.

"Wow!" Katey repeated.

■ ■ ■

The hushed whispers and the noise of the train set from the living room woke Heather upstairs. She knew the children were up and smiled. She nudged her husband.

"Wake up, Jimmy. It's the Christmas *before* the Christmas."

Briscoe slowly woke up. Heather rose and stretched. Putting on her robe, she took a moment to look out the window and saw that it had snowed another foot during the night and the driveway was covered.

"Some 'fine' day to travel to the airport," she murmured glumly.

■ ■ ■

Arm in arm, Briscoe and Heather went downstairs and, as they stood silently in the doorway, watched with delight as Katey and Gilly played with their new treasures.

Gilly saw them. "Look, Mom, Dad! Santa was here and it's not even Christmas!"

"So I see," Heather said.

Gilly asked, "How come? How come he came early?"

Briscoe fielded the question. "Well, I think it's because he heard I was leaving today and he's such a nice guy, you know, so I think he wanted me to watch you two open your presents."

Katey proudly held up her new dress. "Mommy, Santa brought me a pretty velvet dress!"

"It's beautiful, Honey," Heather agreed. "I think you should wear it to Grandma's today."

"I will, I will!" Katey said eagerly.

Briscoe and Heather smiled at each other. Early Christmas was a big success.

■ ■ ■

They finished opening their presents, had breakfast, and then the family dressed for the trip to the airport.

Briscoe rushed into the kitchen carrying his suitcase with Gilly following close behind. The kitchen television set was tuned to The Weather Channel.

"Do you have your passport?" Heather asked him.

Briscoe patted his sport coat pocket. "Yes." He then turned and yelled up the hallway. "Come on, Katey." To Gilly, he said, "Gilly, get your coat."

Briscoe stopped to turn off the television, but paused a moment to listen.

The TV meteorologist reported, "A travel advisory is still in effect, but the main storm that went through the county last night has now passed to the east. There were record cold temperatures last night."

Briscoe nodded. "That's good. Conditions can only get better then."

The TV meteorologist continued, "Today we should see warm temps of two degrees with a wind chill of minus seventeen."

He clicked off the TV just as Katey stepped into the kitchen wearing her new Christmas dress.

"How do I look, Daddy? Mommy helped me put it on."

She stood there, all smiles, with her arms outstretched, looking very much like a child fashion model. The black velvet dress had a white-laced collar with white pearl buttons and a red, plaid satin sash.

"Oh, Sweetheart...you look so beautiful," he said.

Entering the kitchen, Heather said, "Isn't she pretty?"

"An absolute vision!" Briscoe added.

Gilly asked, "What's a vision?"

"Thank you," Katey said.

"Okay, gang, let's go!" Briscoe said, trying to get the family moving. "The airplane's waiting."

■ ■ ■

With coats and gloves in hand, the family hurried into the garage. They locked the house door behind them. Briscoe pressed the automatic door opener and carried his suitcase to the trunk. The garage door opened, revealing a fresh layer of snow that had fallen on the driveway during the day.

"More snow," Briscoe said aloud to himself.

"Jimmy, do you have your ticket?" Heather asked as she walked to the passenger side of the car.

Briscoe patted his coat pocket again. "Yes. Right here; beside my passport."

"And your license?"

"Yes, yes. Stop worrying. I haven't forgotten anything," he said warmly to her. He had forgotten all three documents once ten years ago and this resulted in his missing the flight. Heather had never let him forget it since.

Katey asked, "Daddy, does Santa ever visit the ships?"

As Briscoe opened the trunk, he replied, "He used to, but he doesn't anymore." He placed the suitcase in the trunk and shut the lid.

Gilly was curious, too. "Why not?"

"In the car, kids," he said.

Gilly climbed into the back seat. Briscoe lifted Katey into her car seat and strapped her in. That was when he noticed his daughter's head. "Katey, where's your hat?"

"It's inside," she answered.

"Okay, I'll get it. It's too cold to be outside without it."

Briscoe started for the house door when Heather said, "It's locked, Jimmy. I have the keys here." She reached into her purse.

Briscoe turned and said, "Never mind. Let's go. The car will be warm soon." He climbed into the car.

Gilly repeated his question. "Dad, why not?"

"Why not what?"

"Why doesn't Santa ever visit the ships?"

"Well, I will tell you," Briscoe said as he fastened his seatbelt and started the engine. "There was one year he tried coming down the smoke stack with that big bag of his and he got stuck. He plugged up the exhaust gases and the engines tripped out and the propeller stopped. It was a real mess. The ship drifted for over a week. After that, the company said 'No more Santa on the ships!'"

"What a mean company," Katey commented.

"That's what I say," Heather said dryly with a raised eye, but for different reasons.

Gilly was skeptical. "Daddy, did he *really* get stuck in the smoke stack?"

"Oh, absolutely. You don't believe me? Just call the company sometime and ask them. They'll tell you."

Briscoe backed the white Volvo out of the garage and turned the car around so it was pointing up the steep driveway. He had shoveled the driveway earlier, but it was snowing again and the driveway was covered and slippery. On his first attempt up the driveway, he got a poor start and spun the tires, causing the car to slip sideways.

"Boo!" Katey and Gilly shouted, playfully expressing in unison their disapproval over their dad's driving.

Briscoe immediately took his foot off the accelerator to stop the sideways slide.

"I should have shoveled again," he said.

"Too late now," Heather said, thinking about his flight time.

He then let the Volvo roll backwards to position it for another attempt up the hill. He floored the accelerator and the car raced up the hill. He traveled a little further than before, but then halfway up the driveway the tires spun out again and the car stopped.

"Boo!" the children repeated. They giggled at their father's dilemma.

"Okay," Briscoe sighed. "One more time."

Briscoe backed down the driveway again as far as he could which was nearly into the woods. With another racing start, the car shot up the driveway like a bullet, smashed through the two-foot deep ridge of snow left by the snowplow at the top of the driveway, and onto the main road.

"Yea!" Katey and Gilly cheered.

At that same moment, there was the loud blast of a horn. Briscoe quickly looked over his shoulder and saw that he had nearly collided with a passing snowplow. The snowplow had come to an abrupt halt. The disgruntled driver shook his head.

Heather sighed with relief. "Whew, that was close."

Briscoe waved apologetically at the driver and drove on.

With the journey underway, Heather picked up the cell phone and called her mother.

"Hi, Mom. We're on our way to the airport and then we'll be right over. Probably in an hour and a half. Okay, I will." She looked at Briscoe and said, "Mom says to tell you you're a bum for leaving, but have a safe trip anyway."

"Tell her I said thank you, and a Merry Christmas to you, too," Briscoe said as he drove.

To her mother, Heather asked, "Did you hear that? Okay." She passed the cell phone to the children and said, "Here, kids, talk to Grandma. Tell Grandma we're coming."

Gilly took the phone. "Hi, Grandma. We're coming."

"Let me talk to her!" Katey said excitedly, reaching for the phone from her car seat.

Gilly slid over to his sister's car seat and held the phone to her head.

"Hi, Grandma. I have a new dress. It's really pretty. Wait 'til you see it. Bye."

Gilly returned the phone to his mother.

Heather spoke. "Okay, Mom. That's the story here. We'll be there in a little while. Bye." She pressed the cell phone's hang up button and set it down in the car's console.

Katey watched with interest as she did this. She was always fascinated by the little phone with its glowing numbers.

Gilly changed his line of questioning. "Mommy, is Otto really going to be okay at the doggy hotel while Grandma Louise is visiting during Christmas?"

Heather nodded. "Yes, honey. He'll be fine, and he *likes* going to the doggy hotel because he can have fun with all of his doggy pals."

Katey pursued the train of thought. "Why can't he stay home?"

Heather replied, "Grandma Louise is allergic to dogs."

Gilly knew better. "Grandma Louise doesn't *like* dogs."

"That's not true, Honey," Heather said.

"Grandma Louise is *scared* of big dogs," Briscoe said, jumping into the conversation.

Katey looked sadly at her parents. "Even Otto?"

Heather answered, "Yes, sweetie. Even Otto."

"Poor Otto," the little girl said. She was missing her dog already and he hadn't gone anywhere.

"She'll be fine, sweetie," Heather reassured her.

■ ■ ■

Along a snow-covered, countryside road, the snowfall increased and the visibility began to deteriorate. Briscoe had his headlights on and was driving slow, about 35 mph. With no morning traffic, their Volvo seemed to be the only car on the road and the kids were enjoying the snowy, country ride.

Gilly said, "I can't wait to get to Grandma's. I like her pies."

Noticing her dad was driving slower than usual, Katey asked, "When are we going to get there, Mommy?"

"Right after we drop Daddy off at the airport."

The Volvo approached a bend in the road. Strong gusts of wind blew snow across the road and visibility dropped to about one hundred feet. Heavy drifts had formed along both sides of the road. Briscoe turned the wheel to negotiate the curve...and there was no response.

The children were giggling in the background. Heather felt the car slide.

"Ice," Briscoe said, worried.

Heather was worried, too, as she clutched the handle above the passenger side door. "Jimmy..."

Suddenly, out of the snowfall, headlights appeared. The approaching car had also hit the icy patch in the bend and was out of control.

"No, no, no," Heather said, gripping the handle tighter, terror building.

Gilly and Katey stopped giggling and a look of fear crossed their faces.

Gilly asked, "Dad, what's happening?

There was no time to answer.

In an instant, both cars collided at an oblique angle. The other car had been traveling much faster than they and it smashed them hard. Both cars went over the edge of the country road where they leapt into a violent roll down a steep, thirty-foot embankment.

Heather and Briscoe were whip-lashed sideways on impact. Heather's head slammed hard against the passenger's side window, smashing the glass. Gilly's head was thrown against the rear side door. The baby's seat, with its two over-the-shoulder straps, kept Katey locked snuggly in place.

The bottom of the embankment suddenly leveled off. The Volvo rolled lazily several more times before coming to a rest upside down in an adjacent farmer's field. The other car disappeared in the blinding snow.

Katey shrieked in terror. Her car seat was still buckled and she was hanging upside down. "Mommy! Daddy! Gilly!"

None of her family responded to her cries.

Briscoe, Heather, and Gilly were unconscious and bloody. All of the car's windows were smashed and the blustering wind drove cold air and snow through the car. Katey was terrified and began to cry. She shrieked again. "Mommy! Gilly!"

She waited for an answer and shrieked again. "Daddy! Daddy!"

When there was no response, the little girl continued to cry. It was getting colder and she was terribly frightened in her upside position. Suddenly, a glow from below caught her attention and she looked down at the car's roof. Among the shattered glass, she saw her mother's cell phone lying there. It was still working. Its clock was still keeping time. Katey reached out for it, but it was too far away. It might as well have been on the moon. She tried to unbuckle herself from the car seat, but couldn't. She wasn't strong enough.

All Katey could hear was the wind. She began to cry again.

"Mommy! Daddy! Gilly!"

The snow continued to fall.

Chapter Four

Alone

The world seemed detached and foggy as Briscoe lay half-conscious in a hospital bed. A doctor entered the room and approached him. Briscoe opened his bruised eyes and passively watched him. Was he real or was he a dream? The sharpness of the doctor's image and the clarity of the hospital sounds in the background told him he must be real.

"How are you feeling?" the doctor asked.

Briscoe didn't answer. He couldn't answer. He didn't know.

"Can you talk yet?" the doctor tried again.

Briscoe opened his mouth. No words came out. He merely blinked.

"No?" the doctor asked.

Still, Briscoe could not answer, but kept his eyes on the doctor.

The doctor sensed Briscoe was coming around. This was the most responsive his patient had been in forty-eight hours. Proceeding with great difficulty, the doctor said, "I have to tell you...maybe you already know...Mr. Briscoe, your family...your family didn't survive the accident. I am sorry to have to tell you this."

Briscoe shut his eyes tightly in pain.

■　■　■

Two days later Jimmy Briscoe climbed out of bed.

It had been two, immeasurably long days and nights of guilt, sorrow, and pain. Every moment filled with remorse and self-incrimination. Every second ticking away like drops used in Chinese water torture; his mind unable to escape the self-inflicted, helpless agony. Unsteadily, he limped to the window in his private room. He attempted to open it, but the window was either sealed or he was too weak to open it. He didn't know which. He looked around the room for something heavy. Seeing a desk chair in the corner, he managed to go to it and drag it back to the window. Mustering all of his strength, he picked it up, swung it around, and smashed out the heavy plate of glass. Shattered glass flew everywhere; moments later he could hear the pieces hitting the sidewalk below. Setting the chair down, he leaned it against the glass-covered sill, jagged edges and all. Using the chair as a step, he climbed up onto the sill and stuck his head through the window. He stopped and stared down at the sidewalk eight stories below.

The door to his room opened just then and two nurses rushed in. When they saw him in the window, they froze, dumbfounded by the sight of broken glass everywhere and a badly injured patient leaning precariously out of the eight-story window.

Both nurses remained calm. One nurse finally spoke. She had short, blonde hair and a kindly, caring face. She said to him in a most gentle way, "Please don't."

The desire to end his life came and went. Briscoe knew he didn't have it in his heart. A moment passed and he slowly climbed back into the room, and then moved away from the window. Ashamed and confused, tears running down his cheeks, he looked at both nurses and said, in a voice no louder than a whisper, "I'm sorry I broke it."

"It's okay," the kind nurse said. "It can be fixed."

"I'm sorry," he repeated softly.

"It's okay."

He shook his head as though he didn't know what he must have been thinking, and then quietly returned to bed.

■ ■ ■

The Pristine Funeral Home, an old, renovated Victorian house which had been built in the late 1800's, stood with dignity in the middle of a snow-covered plot of land off the center of downtown Pristine. The property itself was surrounded by a wall of towering, trimmed shrubs that provided privacy from the busy downtown traffic. Like most funeral homes, it was painted a cheery white. Under the gloomy circumstances that usually brought people together beneath the roof of this gabled house, white was a cheery color and, in a subtle, psychological way, aided in diminishing grief.

The house had been renovated several times during its century-old existence, each time adding extra viewing rooms and entrances. In its present state the house could accommodate three different families at the same time and privacy between them easily maintained. For larger viewings the rooms could be opened to one another with folding partitions to form one large room. This was done in the case of the Briscoe family.

The huge room was filled to capacity. James Briscoe sat in the first row with his head down as Reverend Flory delivered the eulogy. Only a few feet away sat his family's caskets, beneath the dim, recessed lights in the ceiling. The caskets were heavy-looking and polished; seemingly fresh from a fine craftsman's workshop; each covered with a lovely spray. There were countless floral arrangements about the room and surrounding the three caskets. Heather's casket sat directly in front of him while his children's were placed at either end of it; Gilly on the right, Katey on the left. Their lids were closed.

The room was unusually warm, Briscoe thought. He was hot and his forehead was moist. He felt slightly dizzy. He reached into his pocket for a handkerchief, but felt something else: Heather's wedding ring.

I Am Yours.

In his pocket was a plastic bag containing the ring. Floyd Gabriel, the owner of the funeral home, had asked him if he had wanted it buried with her. He had said no; that he wanted to keep it in a special place for her. Gabriel had presented it to him just before the eulogy. It was identical to his own. It's inscription read "I Am Yours."

As Reverend Flory spoke, the sounds of weeping surrounded him.

Despite the enormous grief that had engulfed him, Briscoe was surprised at the large turnout of people who had come to grieve his loss. He hadn't realized there were so many people that had known his wife, his kids, and himself. Most of the faces were familiar to him, but he couldn't remember most of their names. He had spent so much of his time away at work and when he returned home from sea, reuniting with his wife and kids encompassed most of his time. Reuniting with his neighbors had always been the last thing to do on his vacation list.

One row behind him Louise Evans, his mother-in-law, sat in angry silence. Her dark, almost blackish eyes were locked firmly onto her son-in-law as Reverend Flory's eulogy continued. She was a stout woman, in her early sixties, her skin prematurely wrinkled due to countless days of sunbathing on the Florida beaches during her youth. Her anger had made her face flush and her skin was so hot that any tears the woman had cried that day had long since evaporated away. There were red lipstick smudges along the edges of her upper and lower incisors - a sure sign that Louise Evans was enraged about something. It was an old habit of hers. Whenever she was upset she'd forget about her lipstick and bite her lips.

Beside her was his father-in-law, Melvin Evans; a small, harmless-looking man with wire-rimmed glasses whose attempts with Grecian Formula on his thinning gray hair had failed. As usual, Melvin's suit was slightly larger than his small build could properly support.

Together, Louise and Melvin made the standard odd-looking couple: he short and meek; she tall and domineering. They looked like the kind of couple that would have absolutely nothing in common. Perhaps for most of their married lives this might have been true, but at that very moment they did have something in common: they both had lost their only daughter along with their only grandchildren.

As they sat listening to the Reverend's eulogy, Melvin appeared quiet and stunned; his face pale and empty; a man devastated by events beyond his control. Louise, on the other hand, was very much alive and breathing rapidly. The heat radiated from her broad, leathery face and her hands trembled as she fought to control herself. She looked like a nuclear reactor about ready to explode.

Reverend Flory was a congenial man with a short clipped mustache and had known the Briscoes for years. He stood behind the small podium and, speaking articulately, spread generous words of consolation to the large group of grief-stricken friends and relatives that had gathered.

Briscoe listened to Flory's voice without really hearing his words or his gentle thoughts. The voice had been the same voice that had joined Heather and he in holy matrimony ten years before. He stared at Heather's coffin and thought of the past, which up until only last week didn't seem that long ago. Now the past seemed like an eternity gone by. Death, because of its finality, had a way of severely cutting the past off from the present. Those moments with Heather and the kids were now gone forever. Heather and the kids would no longer be there to help him keep the past alive. They would only live inside his memories.

Before Briscoe knew it, Reverend Flory was finished with the eulogy. People quietly stood and prepared to leave. Flory walked up to him, took his hand into his own, and said, "I'm so sorry, James."

Reverend Flory had always called him "James."

"Thank you, Reverend Flory," Briscoe said.

Behind him, the steaming volcano called Louise Evans finally exploded.

"This wouldn't have happened if you hadn't been traipsing all over the world," she declared as friends and visitors were leaving.

Melvin took her arm gently and spoke. "Dear, take it easy. Control yourself."

"Take it easy?" she cried, jerking her arm out of his grip and shoving him aside. "My daughter and my grandson were killed, and my granddaughter froze to death! And you tell me to take it easy?" She again seared Briscoe with a fiery gaze and asked, "You were behind the wheel!"

Briscoe was shocked. "Froze to death?" he asked, his jaw dropping. He hadn't been told this. All he had been told was they had all died of injuries suffered in the crash.

There was a gasp amongst the crowd of visitors who could do nothing but helplessly stand around and listen. Many others hadn't known the fate of little Katey as well.

"Louise!" Melvin said, raising his voice.

Louise Evans saw the revelation stun Briscoe and cause him great pain. It was as though he had been stabbed through the heart with a knife. At that moment she relished it.

"Yes! She *froze* to death!" Louise continued, turning the knife in Briscoe's heart. "They said she had laid there strapped in her car seat for hours!"

Briscoe helplessly looked at Reverend Flory. "Why didn't anyone tell me?"

Reverend Flory shook his head. He hadn't known either.

Briscoe looked at Floyd Gabriel, the owner of the funeral home.

"Jimmy, she's hysterical," Gabriel said.

"Is it true?" Briscoe demanded.

Gabriel lowered his head and reluctantly nodded.

"Why didn't anyone tell me?" he demanded.

"Because they wanted *us* - the family - to tell *you* in good time," Louise shouted at the top of her lungs. "And now I'm *telling* you. They didn't tell you because they 'didn't want to upset you any more than you were,'" she said in a mocking voice. "Bullshit! As if you really cared!"

"Louise, stop it," Melvin pleaded. To Briscoe, "She doesn't mean it, Jimmy."

Briscoe was no longer listening to either Melvin or his mother-in-law's tirade. "Katey froze to death," he muttered to himself. "Oh God."

"Please, please," Reverend Flory said, trying to calm the situation. "We've all been under a great deal of strain."

A moment later Louise Evans collapsed in one of the pews and cried to herself.

"Please, Jimmy, please," Melvin said trying to apologize for his wife. "Ignore Louise. She's not herself. She's in a state of shock."

"Who the hell isn't?" Briscoe said, bewildered, his voice shaky.

He hurried out of the funeral home and went to his own home - with it on his mind.

Katey froze to death.

■ ■ ■

Katey froze to death.

The usually warm Briscoe kitchen seemed cold to Briscoe now. He sat alone at the kitchen table with a bottle of Johnny Walker Black, a half-full glass, and several photo albums scattered in front of him. Beside the bottle of Scotch lay Heather's wedding band. Otto was lying under the table at his feet. The house was so unbearably quiet. It was suddenly a house full of memories of a former life. Briscoe looked at the photos; pictures of last Halloween, and the cutting of the Christmas tree gazed up at him.

Katey froze to death.

The thought ate away at him.

She must have been terrified and crying. Why didn't I wake to her cries?

The silence was broken with the ringing of the telephone.

Briscoe ignored it and turned a page in the album. A moment later an answering machine in the den intercepted the call. He winced briefly when he heard Heather's upbeat voice on the answering tape.

"Hi! This is Heather. I can't come to the phone right now. Please leave a message and I'll call you as soon as I can. Thank you."

The answering machine toned.

The distress-laden voice of his friend Barney Hubbard came over the speaker.

"Jimmy...this is Barney. Marilee and I just heard. I...I'm so sorry. If there's anything we can do, just let us know. I'll try calling again later. Take care, Buddy."

Click.

That's right, he thought. *Barney is home from the ship.* It was the first time since the tragedy occurred that Briscoe had thought of Barney and Marilee. Someone else was out filling in for him on the *Majestic Prince*. It had been Marilee's life-threatening delivery which had prompted him to return to work early in the first place; the reason he and the family were heading to the airport and out on that treacherous road.

It's not your fault, Barney, Marilee. It's not your fault.

Briscoe flipped another page in the album. A photo of Katey stared back at him.

The happy child was standing with her arm around Pluto at Disney World. Cinderella's castle stood proudly in the background.

"My little baby girl," he said to Otto. "The kid's car seat did what it was supposed to do. The good ol' kid's car seat saved her life, Otto."

Otto raised his head as he always did when he heard his name spoken.

"What good did it do her? She *froze* to death."

He turned another page of the scrapbook and found a bathing suit clad Heather smiling up at him. He then glanced at Heather's wedding band lying beside the glass of Scotch. He picked it up and studied it. The inscription "I Am Yours" twinkled in the light.

"I am unworthy of this."

The dog cocked his head in befuddlement.

31

The telephone rang again just then and the answering machine took the call. Heather's happy greeting played again and the machine toned.

"Jimmy, this is Brenda. Tommy and I just wanted to let you know that if there's anything we can do for you over there... Well, you know where you can find us. Bye."

Click.

"I don't need anything," he said to himself.

He put his glass down and stood up. Briscoe walked into the den and turned off the answering machine. He couldn't bear to hear Heather's voice again. As he passed the den bookcase, more family photos caught his eye. Pictures of the kids and Heather at different places at different times. Happy faces. Fun-filled pictures. Snapshots of life. Happy places. *Katey froze to death.* Happy family. Happy Katey. Katey and Gilly. *Katey froze to death.*

"I should be with them."

Otto wandered into the den just then. The sheepdog sat down beside him and began to whine.

Briscoe looked at the dog and said, "I know, Otto. I miss them, too."

He knelt down and gave the fluffy dog a big hug.

"You're all I have left, boy."

■ ■ ■

The days passed. The sun rose, and then the sun set. The days following the funeral seemed to go by without direction for Jimmy Briscoe.

He wandered around the silent house aimlessly looking at the objects that had accumulated over the decade of their marriage. The pieces of furniture and the antiques; the clothing; the toys in the kids' rooms; the little touches here and there that make a home a home. Each item, important or insignificant, sentimental or utilitarian, that had entered their home had its own history. Where it was bought, why they had needed or wanted it, the discussions and the decision-making process that had gone into the purchase, whether or not they could have afforded it, the actual trip to somewhere to buy it. Some things he remembered clearly; others nagged at him, trying to jar his memory.

The history of his family lie in front of him and, like an archaeologist sifting through ancient ruins, he tried to remember every little thing, every moment about his family; about the past life he had just led.

The sun rose, and then the sun set.

Chapter Five

Return to the Majestic Prince

Months later and on the other side of the world, thirteen time zones away, the 747 flight touched down at KIX. Kansai International Airport. Once Briscoe made it through customs, a Japanese shipping services agent met and escorted him to the Osaka Gas Terminal at Senboku. Thirty minutes later, with his suitcase in hand, Briscoe walked down the long dock toward his ship, the *Majestic Prince*. He walked along the dock with the enthusiasm of a prisoner returning from a weekend furlough. His well-trained, chief mate's eye automatically surveyed the condition of the ship. It was an old habit. He noted the vessel's draft: Thirty-two feet forward; thirty-five feet, nine inches aft. As he crossed the gangway and boarded, he noted that the huge, spherical cargo tank number five - "ball five," to the crew - needed chipping and priming. He then noticed the safety lines, made up and tied to the railing at the top of the tank. The bosun and the gang were already working on ball five. The valves on the dry chemical fire extinguishing system at tank three needed a coat of grease. The fore and aft gas pipeline was in good condition. The nitrogen tank light was out. And so on. With every step, his eyes took pictures and his brain automatically processed what needed to be done in the upcoming weeks. He almost felt like a robot.

Upon entering Captain Tyler Leech's office, Leech appeared uncharacteristically concerned. It was obvious to Briscoe that the captain knew of his tragedy.

"Mr. Bris-coe... I heard from the office what happened to you and your family. I didn't think you'd come back to sea."

Briscoe shook his head. "I almost didn't, sir. But...it was time to get out of the house and work again."

"Words cannot express how terribly sorry I am."

"Thank you, Captain."

Leech continued. "I am truly sorry. I know how you must feel. It is a terrible thing, James, to lose one's family. We go to sea, we leave our loved ones behind in order to provide for them, and we hope they'll be safe. And for most of us, nothing ever happens. But for a few of us, it does. I know. I know very well. I lost my own family thirty years ago."

Briscoe was surprised. "I didn't know."

"It was a long time ago. I never remarried."

Briscoe nodded, understanding why one wouldn't.

Leech held out a pen for him above the shipping articles. Before assuming any position aboard ship, all crewmembers had to sign the articles.

Briscoe took the pen. He paused for a moment, wondering if he really wanted to be back onboard; to return to sea.

What else can I do?

The errant thought passed. He then located his typewritten name among the list of crewmembers and then placed his signature beside it. He was now officially a crewmember once again on the *Majestic Prince.*

"Captain...I, ah, would prefer that no one knows about it. I don't want people to feel pity or sympathy or anything that would get in the way of me doing my job. I'd appreciate it if you wouldn't mention it to anyone."

"Most of the officers know already, James. After all, you were off work for many months. You know how it is. When an officer doesn't return, everyone wants to know why. Most of the crew, however, are new and probably don't know."

Briscoe nodded.

"Welcome back."

"Thank you, sir."

The next morning the mooring wires were let go. Four, large tugs pushed the great ship off the Osaka Gas Terminal dock and turned her around. The *Majestic Prince* headed down Osaka Bay and then out to sea to continue her dedicated shuttle run, hauling liquefied natural gas between Indonesia and Japan.

35

■ ■ ■

It was two weeks after Briscoe returned to work that the birthday party for one of the crewmembers was held in Steward Stancy's room on the 02 deck. It was a fun-filled affair with loud music. Most of the off-duty, unlicensed crew took part in it at some point during the evening. Among those crewmembers present was Darryl Hawkins.

Darryl "the Kid" Hawkins was fresh out of Maryland's Piney Point sailor factory and was the ship's only ordinary seaman. An eager newcomer to the sea, he knew very little about the effects of a single beer on his body chemistry. After one beer, the effects of it kicked in his "autopilot."

His autopilot told him he should spice up this dying party a bit with some entertainment and it thereby directed him to eat an entire bag of potato chips. He did so and then chased them down with the cellophane bag in which they had been packaged. This feat caught the attention of everyone in the room and it wasn't long before he was the focal point of attention. Everyone was daring him to consume something else. Steward Stancy produced a bottle of Tabasco sauce from the galley. Darryl drank it in seconds and tossed the empty bottle in the trash basket. George Mellon, the fifty-three year-old seaman, handed him a crab. Darryl ate the entire thing - shell and all. Someone handed him a box of Ritz crackers and he consumed every last cracker, and then went on to eat the cardboard box as well. There was a boisterous round of applause at each of these most truly amazing feats. No longer hungry, and in need of new frontiers to pioneer, Darryl then changed his act and climbed up on top of Steward Stancy's desk where he began dancing in a wild, frenzied manner, totally out of synch with the rhythms pouring out of the ghetto blaster, while downing a second can of beer.

"Be careful, Darryl," someone called. "You don't want to fall."

"Better get the ship's straitjacket! The Kid's going bananas!" Mellon exclaimed.

"Man, what a cheap drunk he is!" someone else observed.

"Quick! Someone call Bosun Knuckles! Tell him the Kid's *aloft* on the desk."

"Tell him he's aloft in the *head*!"

Darryl instantly took offense to the remark and his Saturday night fever fizzled out. The word "aloft" stabbed into his brain and his autopilot began directing his thoughts in an entirely different direction: the ship's cargo tank covers.

The *Majestic Prince's* main cargo containment system consisted of five enormous, spherical aluminum tanks, each one was one hundred and twenty feet in diameter. Half of each sphere was hidden below the main deck. The other half was protected by a steel-plated, semi-spherical shell with an apex reaching sixty feet above the main deck. These were the ship's cargo tank covers.

Bosun Knuckles considered Darryl Hawkins a clumsy, unreliable fellow. He wouldn't trust him to paint from a six-foot step ladder much less make sixty-foot painting descents down the sides of the spherical covers in a bosun's chair. Darryl's shipmates chided him frequently about Knuckles' lack of confidence, especially when it came to the bosun's chair. The bosun's chair was among the simplest pieces of gear that was standard on all ships and was used for work aloft. It consisted of a short, wooden board which served as a "chair" for the seaman to sit, with a rope bridle spliced around it. The bridle was then secured to a lowering line. Knuckles had no faith at all that Darryl could work with such a simple thing.

Needing still more frontiers to conquer, Darryl's autopilot decided that the young, black man should demonstrate his ability, prove his manhood, and establish once and for all that he was entirely capable and trustworthy of making a drop down the side of a cargo tank. After all, descending down a cargo tank was a right of passage for every new sailor that joined an LNG ship and Darryl Hawkins was not about to let this golden opportunity slip away. Not only would he prove once and for all - to all - that he could indeed make the drop, but he would do it during the *blackness* of the night! An unprecedented act throughout the entire GascoTrans fleet! It had never been done before! No one would ever question his competency again. He would make seagoing history!

Or he would get fired and be barred from the fleet. Was it worth the risk?

Yes! That is what Darryl Hawkins' misguided autopilot fed his receptive mind during those moments after the word "aloft" spilled from someone's lips during the party. He immediately bolted from Steward Stancy's room.

"Hey, 'Kid,' where ya going?" George Mellon called out, but received no reply.

He was long gone.

"I've never seen anyone get so wound up on just two beers before," Steward Stancy said to Mellon.

"Ah, he's always like that," Mellon said, and then downed another beer.

■ ■ ■

Darryl dashed down to the bosun's locker on the main deck and grabbed a safety harness, a shackle, and a spring-loaded anti-fall protector. He then lugged all of this equipment up the center stairs within the house and all the way up to the 05 deck.

The 05 deck. The catwalk deck! The top of the cargo tanks!

Hauling his gear and dragging his safety harness behind him, Darryl strode forward onto the catwalk. The catwalk was a narrow, three-foot wide, bridge-like structure that connected the tops of the five spherical cargo tanks. Its span was seventy feet above the main deck. It was dark out and Darryl had to feel his way around the top of tank five, the aftermost and closest tank to the house. He didn't want to use a flashlight because tank five was directly in front of and below the navigation bridge. A flashlight on top of tank five would instantly cause attention and end his attempt for fame.

No flashlight tonight. No way, man! Darryl Hawkins is too smart for that, he said to himself.

Stepping out onto the top of the tank cover, Darryl could barely make out the nylon drop lines in the shadows. The painting of tank five had been going on for the last three weeks and to save time every morning rigging the drop lines, Bosun Knuckles merely left the lines out during the night. They were coiled and secured to the guardrail that encircled the dome's top.

Darryl stepped into his safety harness, tightened the belt around his waist, and buckled it. He then took both of the drop lines, untied them from the guardrail and, with one end of each still secured to the railing, tossed them down the side of the tank where they stretched out and touched the main deck. He took one of the lines in hand, unscrewed the pin on the shackle, passed a cat's paw over it, and replaced the pin. With the main line secured, he then went about the business of securing his safety line. He took the anti-fall protector, clipped it to his harness, and then clamped the one-way device onto the second nylon line. The anti-fall protector was a device which allowed only one-way movement along a safety line. The trick was making sure you had the device right side up.

Ha! he thought. *I know it works only one-way. And I know which way to set it so that it keeps me from falling. Ha! Some fools rig it upside down and it doesn't do 'em one bit of good except get 'em splattered all over the deck when they fall. Ha!*

No matter how misguided his autopilot was acting that night, Darryl had done a perfect rigging job on both lines. He then climbed over the guardrail and began his first descent down the side of the tank.

Whoopee! Darryl, my main man, you're going down! Ha-ha! I'll show that old, craggy bosun!

Darryl carefully passed more slack though his cat's paw and shackle and then released the anti-fall device to pass more slack through it, working both lines, one at a time, thus inching his way safely down the curved side of the huge tank. He was doing great and enjoying the moment. But...

...he didn't see the pad eye.

Pad eyes were small steel plates, welded to the tank cover and pointed straight up, three inches into the air. They had a hole drilled through them and allowed the attachment of rigging and shackles. They were everywhere on the tank cover and had been there since the days of the ship's construction when they were used to lower the massive tank covers into place over the enormous, aluminum ball cargo tanks.

Darryl didn't see the pad eye and tripped over it. One moment he was standing up lowering himself down the curved side of the tank in an expert manner, happy and proud as a lark; the next moment he found himself tumbling and upside down like a turtle on his back, his head pointing dizzyingly downward toward the main deck fifty feet below.

Helpless and frightened, Darryl began screaming for help.

■ ■ ■

The next morning Briscoe sat at his desk quietly sipping on his first cup of coffee of the day. His short-wave radio was on and a *Voice of America* newscast was in progress telling a story about a plane crash somewhere in the world. He let the morning's *VOA* news slip in one ear and out the other, and then glanced at his watch. It said two minutes to eight. Briscoe pushed the troublesome news story to the back of his mind for there were other matters on hand to deal with that morning. Captain Leech had called and was expecting him in his office at eight o'clock sharp to discuss the Darryl Hawkins and George Mellon incidents.

After one round-trip to Indonesia and back to Japan, Briscoe knew the tour would not be scot-free of personnel problems. The deck and engine officers were a decent lot. He had sailed with all of the officers many times before, except third mate Philip Short who was the new kid on the block. The ABs in his department, on the other hand, were a mixed bunch. In a ship's hierarchy, the ABs, or able-bodied seamen, were unlicensed individuals who worked for the chief mate and bosun on deck performing routine maintenance jobs and whose duties on the bridge included lookout and helmsman. There were six on this ship, and after a week onboard, Briscoe had sized up his AB's abilities and noted their problems.

On the dark side, he had Clarke Bickle and Arnie Dell. Both were lazy when it came to work and both tended to be smart mouths. For all Briscoe knew, they could have been brothers. On the bright side of the deck department, he had Bosun Billy Knuckles, and ABs Max Hillert, Mo Silalahi, and John O'Connell. Knuckles was the best bosun that could be found anywhere, and Hillert, Silalahi, and O'Connell were highly competent, reliable, and professional sailors.

In the middle of both extremes, lay AB George Mellon and ordinary seaman Darryl Hawkins. Mellon was, at fifty-three, strong, burly, experienced, and a hard-worker. However, he had been a problem drinker since he returned to the ship and Briscoe knew it was only a matter of time before the veteran seaman would lose his job. Captain Leech had already given him his first (and last) warning.

Darryl Hawkins, the black OS, was an energetic newcomer and the *Majestic Prince* was his first ship. He was so eager to perform and do well that it frequently got him into trouble. He tended to do things on his own without anyone's permission or supervision. Since returning to the ship Briscoe had cautioned the young man on two occasions that his "loose cannon" style aboard the ship was a detriment rather than an asset and would be his downfall.

As he sipped his coffee, Briscoe knew Mellon was history. Intoxicated, Mellon had stumbled up to the bridge for watch last night and the mate on duty turned him right around and sent him to his room. Since showing up intoxicated for bridge watch was a firing offense, that incident was cut and dry. Leech never deviated from that rule unless the chief mate could provide strong arguments on behalf of a man. In Mellon's case, Briscoe had no desire to go to bat for the man, and, in fact, was happy to see him go.

However, the Hawkins incident was different and was causing him concern that morning. Leech had learned of the Hawkins incident from Chief Jacobi just before breakfast. Jacobi had called him to complain that his "sleep had been interrupted during the wee hours of the night by all of the activity that the deck department was engaged in up on tank five."

Swell, Briscoe had thought, sipping his coffee. *The cantankerous chief had to slip in there and tell the Old Man before I had a chance. Now the Old Man will think I wasn't going to inform him; that I was out to "protect" the man.*

Briscoe knew he was right. He knew his reputation for fairness when it came to dealing with the crew had cost him occasional points with Captain Leech, and that Leech regarded him with cautious respect. Leech was of the old school of thought that dictated that the officers shall not associate with the crew and to get rid of problem people from the get-go. Period.

Briscoe knew the meeting at eight was not going to be pleasant. He swallowed the last of his coffee, got up from his seat, and headed down the passageway for the Old Man's office.

■ ■ ■

When Briscoe arrived, Captain Leech was standing behind his desk, his hands clasped behind his back, his head raised high so that he could look down his large nose at his chief mate. It was obvious to Briscoe that Leech was not at all happy. They didn't call him "Hire'm Fire'm Leech" for nothing. His staid and arrogant stance made him seem taller and more intimidating than his six-foot two-inch height. His ruddy, sixty-six year-old face was leathery and lined, with a weather-beaten look.

Leech gazed coldly at Briscoe through squinted eyes and said, "Mr. Bris-coe..."

His deep and raspy voice always pronounced Briscoe's name as though it were composed of two words - *Bris Coe* - and then paused briefly, as though he were about to make an important announcement to a large gathering.

"...I would like *your* explanation as to what happened last night. I would also like to know why I had to hear about the incident from Chief Jacobi and not yourself?"

Unaffected by Leech's touchy demeanor, Briscoe said, "Captain, I was planning to inform you of the incident this morning. I didn't think the matter important enough to disturb you from a good night's sleep. The bridge notified me as soon as they heard the trouble on tank five and I rounded up the bosun and a couple of ABs to assist me. The man was not injured and we recovered him off of tank five without any problems."

"How is it that the man came to be in such a precarious position?" Leech asked.

"The bosun has not been comfortable with the idea of letting Hawkins go down the side of the tank and has refused to let him do so. And then last night, it's my understanding that Hawkins apparently felt he wanted to prove that he could do it. He got a little carried away, sir."

"I see. What about alcohol? Was it a factor?"

"I don't think so, Captain. He passed the breathalyzer test."

"Was Mellon involved in this?"

"No, sir. His claim to fame last night was showing up drunk for watch. Again, the bridge notified me. I tried to Breathalyzer him, but he refused. I informed him if he refused, he would be fired. He still refused."

Leech paused for a moment and then said in his usual phlegmatic manner. "I will discharge Mr. Mellon for cause then."

"Yes, Captain, I think that's a good idea."

"And I will discharge Mr. Hawkins for cause, as well. The cause being that he was a safety menace to himself as well as to the crewmembers who were involved in his rescue. I also am going to stop the beer sales in the slop chest immediately."

"Captain, I'm not so sure those two actions are truly necessary. Hawkins is a young man, practically a boy, who still has a lot to learn, I'll agree. He's eager to prove himself. Deep down inside I feel he has the potential to become a first rate seaman and an asset to this ship and the company. This is his first, major screw-up since he's been aboard. I think he should be given another chance. And as far as stopping the beer sales in the slop chest, I don't believe it would be fair to penalize the entire crew for one man's error."

Leech contemplated his chief mate's opinions. "All right, Mr. Bris-coe. I'll only log Mr. Hawkins this time since you feel so strongly about his potential. And I'll leave the beer privileges in the slop chest as they are - for now."

"Thank you, sir."

Leech then grumbled something unintelligible which signaled a reluctant end to the discussion.

Sam's short and stubby body made an appearance in the doorway just then. He had a bent cigarette dangling from his lips and a weather map in his hand. It was fresh off the fax machine. He stepped into Leech's office and handed it to him. "No tropical depressions or typhoons this trip, Captain."

"Glad to hear it. Thank you, Sparks," Leech said looking at the map.

"You're welcome," Sam said. As he turned to leave, he stopped and asked, "Oh, by the way, did you two hear on *Voice of America* this morning about that JAL DC-10 going down at Narita?"

"No," Leech said with mild interest.

"It was a doozy!'

The *Majestic Prince* and the other LNG carriers of the GascoTrans fleet shuttled back and forth between Indonesia and Japan. The American-built ships never returned to the States and all crewmembers joining the GascoTrans fleet flew through either Tokyo's Narita Airport or Osaka's Kansai International Airport to meet the vessels. Since flying to and from Japan was their only link with their homes in the U.S., there was always a more than passing interest in any air disaster that occurred in Japan.

"VOA said the pilot freaked out during the last few seconds before touchdown and reversed the engines. The plane just dropped out of the sky and crashed into Tokyo Bay. Fifty-three people were killed."

"What was wrong with the pilot?" Briscoe asked.

"All they said was he had some mental problems or something."

Sam then disappeared and Briscoe asked, "Is there anything more, Captain?"

"The loggings will be conducted after coffee time this morning. Be sure you have the bosun, Mr. Mellon, and Mr. Hawkins up here at that time. I'll have Sam send a message to the office and order a replacement AB. That'll be all."

"Yes, sir," Briscoe said, and then left.

Leech grumbled to himself again and stepped into his bedroom where he sat down in his recliner, turned on his radio, and listened to *Voice of America.*

■ ■ ■

Later that morning Darryl Hawkins was logged for being a safety hazard. He was given a written warning and told that if he ever was logged again, for anything, it would be the last time he would ever see the *Majestic Prince* or any other GascoTrans vessel again.

George Mellon was fired and removed from all of his remaining shipboard duties. His pay stopped that day and he had nothing to do but sit in his room for the remainder of the trip north and think about where he would find his next job.

■ ■ ■

It was a Briscoe policy to try to help the new, fresh-out-of-sailor-school crewmembers with their shipboard problems before their career opportunities were vaporized by a youthful act of stupidity. With someone as troublesome as Darryl Hawkins, he made no exception. Later that day after the logging, he had "the Kid" sent up to his office.

Darryl, a broad, five-foot-nine, black man of nineteen, sauntered into the office and plopped himself down on the settee. His shoulders drooped and his head leaned lazily over to one side. He was a man with a chip on his shoulder.

44

"Everyone seems to have a complaint about you," Briscoe began. "The second mate says you hung up on him the other morning as he tried to explain your lookout duties over the telephone. The third mate says that during the last undocking you had to be told what to do every step of the way and that you didn't jump in and help your shipmates stow the lines. He says you hung back to the side and watched. The bosun doesn't trust you and thinks you're a safety hazard. He says he can't leave you alone for a minute and that he has to watch you all of the time. And, now, this stunt you pulled last night on tank five has got everyone upset. So, what's your problem, Darryl? Are you *trying* to lose your job?"

Darryl's head straightened up. "No, sir, Mate. I don't know what all of these people are so upset about. Everyone's out to get me."

"That's baloney, Darryl," Briscoe scoffed. "No one's out to get you."

"The second mate, I thought he was finished talking to me and so I hung up. The undocking, well, I was waiting for the third mate to give me an order. And the bosun, he always is hassling me, not letting me do anything. And I really want to help. Last night I wanted to prove I could rig my gear and go down the tank all by myself."

Briscoe said, "When someone is talking to you on the phone, you better make damn sure they're finished before you hang up. During an undocking, if you see everyone else working then you should be working, too. You shouldn't be standing around waiting for the third mate to hand you an invitation. And as far as the bosun is concerned, you're going to have to gain his confidence. You have to prove to him one step at a time that you are trustworthy and can do the job. And if you don't know how to gain his trust, then ask him what you can do to get it."

"I'm trying, Mate. I am."

"Maybe you're trying too hard and aren't thinking your actions through. Now, Darryl, I've stuck up for you each time only because I think you have some potential and each time you've let me down. This is the *last* time I'm going to help you. You could have killed yourself last night. Next time you screw up I'm going to have you thrown off the vessel for good. The Old Man wanted to do it this morning, but I talked him out of it. You let me down again and I may even have your Coast Guard papers pulled."

"You can do that?" the young man asked, astonished.

45

"You better believe I can," Briscoe answered emphatically. Actually, only the Coast Guard had the power to pull a man's papers, but Briscoe wagered the young, ordinary seaman wouldn't know that.

Darryl sat quietly pondering his future if his papers were pulled. He'd have to find a new line of work. His maritime career would be finished.

Briscoe used the moment to take a book out of his bookcase. He placed it on the corner of his desk in front of the ordinary.

"Listen, Darryl, you could become a really good seaman if you worked hard at it. You're strong, you're willing, and you have a few more brain cells than the average bear. Now, all you have to do is put all these good things together and make them work for you. I want you to take this," he said gesturing to the book.

"What is it, Mate?"

"It's the *American Merchant Seaman's Manual.* It's the Bible of all merchant seaman. I want you to take it and read it. Everything's in it. How to splice wire and rope; info about blocks and tackles, paints, lookout duties. Everything. All the basics are there. It will even tell you the rules of the road, how to navigate, and how to treat appendicitis. Anything you want to know. You read the *Manual* from cover to cover and I guarantee you'll be prepared for anything that can happen to you at sea. Anything."

Except the loss of your family, an errant thought flashed through his mind.

Katey froze to death.

"Here take it," Briscoe said, shaking the thought.

"Gee, mate, I've only got a few more trips left before my tour's up and then I'm gone," Darryl said. "I'll never finish reading it."

"That's okay. Read what you can while you're here and then pick one up when you get home. You show me that you really want to keep this job and I'll help you as much as I can. Otherwise you're finished for good. Last chance. Got it?"

"Got it. I'll try. Thanks, Mate," the ordinary said gratefully as he stood and picked up the book. He then headed for the door.

"Darryl," Briscoe said, stopping him.

"Yes, Mate?"

"I looked at the rigging job you did on your harness last night." Giving credit where credit was due, he said to the ordinary, "You did a good job. It saved your life."

Darryl smiled. "Thanks."

"I'll ask the bosun to let you make a drop today."

"All right! Thanks, Mate," Darryl said excitedly, and left with the *Seaman's Manual*.

Chapter Six

Greta Moxey

The next day, Sam happily strolled down the passageway with a telex in his hand. Briscoe was quietly working at his desk when Sam knocked and entered.

"Jimmy, here's a 'terribly important' message from the office. They want to know how much A4-sized copier paper we have on board."

"Thanks, Sam. Just throw it in the tray."

"Also, the crew replacement list came in. Looks like you're getting a female AB to replace Mellon."

"Good," Briscoe acknowledged with indifference. "Just throw it in the tray."

Sam placed the messages in the incoming mail tray on the corner of Briscoe's desk and turned to leave. Feeling sorry for his friend, he stopped and said, "Jimmy...why don't you let me fix you up with an Indonesian girl."

Briscoe looked up from his paperwork. "What?"

"Come ashore with me and I'll get you fixed up."

"No, thanks, Sam. I don't have much desire to get mixed up with anyone."

"Well, nobody said you had to get *involved* with anyone, Jimmy. I'm just saying why don't you go out and get laid."

"Sam, will you quit trying to play the matchmaker," Briscoe said blandly. "I have no desire to go off and play with your girlfriends."

"A strong, virile, young man like you? With no desire? That's impossible. You're bullshitting yourself, Jimmy. Abstinence will not do the dead a bit of good."

Briscoe looked at him with a raised eye and then shrugged.

The sixty-three year-old radio officer said dreamily, "Oh, yes, just think of it: the feel of a nice...soft...young...naked Indonesian girl wrapped around you like a warm blanket; eagerly taking good care of your every wish and need; her curious fingers and wet tongue traveling up and down your body."

"I get the picture. I don't need your porn novel descriptions."

"It might help you forget, Jimmy."

Briscoe said, "I don't want to forget."

Sam was persistent. "You can't spend the rest of your life punishing yourself. I've been watching you these last two months and it's downright pitiful to see you so depressed. The last thing you are, Jimmy Briscoe, is a saint. None of us are. We're just a bunch of human beings. We're all screwed-up in one way or another. We make our mistakes, we learn from them, and then we go on. Besides, Heather probably would have wanted you to go out and have some fun instead of sit around and mope all day. Now, what do you say? Let me fix you up."

"If I change my mind, I'll let you know," Briscoe said appreciatively. "Thanks."

Sam nodded and left. Briscoe glanced at the calendar on his desk and crossed off the days. Beside the calendar were photos of Heather. His eyes shifted to them, and then he returned to his work.

■ ■ ■

It was a clear, July morning when the *Majestic Prince* arrived at the Osaka Gas Terminal with its cargo of 125,000 cubic meters of cryogenic cargo. With the assistance of four powerful tugs, the *Prince* was slowly and gently pushed alongside the dock. Her twelve, heavy, one-and-a-half-inch diameter, stainless steel mooring wires were then made fast to the shoreside mooring hooks. The shoreside gangway was lowered like a castle's drawbridge and set aboard. Once aboard, the usual flurry of in-port activity began.

The shoreside connecting crew, consisting of a twenty-man Japanese team, was the first group of anxiously waiting visitors to board the ship. They headed straight for the ship's loading manifold located between cargo tanks two and three to make the piping connections with the terminal's chicksan arms. The chicksan arms were the movable link in this permanent ship-shore pipeline arrangement. They were designed to accommodate many different types of LNG carriers that visited the terminal, as well to flex and move in harmony with the various tidal conditions that occurred throughout the day. The shipside piping connections consisted of five, stainless steel lines, each sixteen-inches in diameter. They were secured to the terminal's chicksan arms by sixteen stainless steel bolts per pipe. Time at this dock was money and the specialized team that boarded was capable of performing this job in less than fifty minutes.

A horde of other people followed the connection crew: ship's supply personnel delivering food and stores for another voyage; VIPs from the GascoTrans Osaka office to discuss new company policy changes with Captain Leech; cargo gauging personnel to officially measure and document the amount of cargo on board; Japanese interpreters to aid Briscoe in his communications with the Japanese terminal personnel; the ship's agents bringing aboard the crew mail and other ship's business documents; the usual assortment of customs and immigrations officials to clear the vessel. There was also a group of twelve Japanese observers from the Osaka terminal who were there to witness the cargo discharge and ballasting operation from the ship's Cargo Control Room. The CCR, as it was called, was quickly swamped with people for it was the ship's nerve center when in port.

All in all, it was another busy, yet routine day in port for Briscoe and the crew of the *Majestic Prince.*

■　■　■

A short time later another ship's agent arrived with the crew reliefs. One of the reliefs was able-bodied seaman Greta Moxey. Moxey was short - five-six - but she walked tall with her head held high. She carried herself with the self-assuredness and dignity that only a woman who knew who she was, where she was going, and what she wanted would know. It was her third tour aboard an LNG carrier and the size of the ship or its cargo no longer impressed her.

The other relief was a new steward's assistant named Jack Mahoney. Mahoney was, like Darryl Hawkins, a young, nineteen year-old, fresh out of the Piney Point, Maryland sailor factory. It was his first time aboard a ship. Moxey could tell because he had that "totally lost" expression stretched across his face. It was obvious he was awestruck by the sheer size of this liquefied gas carrier.

Once across the gangway, Moxey stopped by the AB on gangway watch. She put down her luggage in front of the watch podium and pleasantly said, "Hi. I'm Greta Moxey."

The AB on watch, Clarke Bickle, glanced up from the book he was reading. Annoyed at the interruption, he gave the young woman the once-over. Realizing she was attractive, he put down his book. He then picked up a pen and opened the gangway logbook.

"Nice to meet you, Greta. I'm Clarke. Clarke Bickle," the AB said, his annoyance melting away as he scribbled her name down in the logbook.

"Nice to meet you, Clarke," Moxey said, noticing the change in the man's attitude. She also noticed he had misspelled her name. "It's spelled X-E-Y. Not X-I-E," she corrected him. "X-I-E is the soft drink."

He shrugged. "Oh, sorry. No one ever reads this thing anyway," he said, not bothering to correct it.

"Where can I find the chief mate?"

"Up there in the CCR."

"Thanks," she said, and she headed for the CCR.

"You're welcome," Bickle replied, giving her another once-over.

"Where do I go?" asked the new steward's assistant.

"You go aft and see the steward and the captain," Moxey said helpfully.

"What's your name?" Bickle asked the young man.

"Jack Mahoney."

Bickle scribbled the name sloppily down in the logbook as Mahoney the new SA headed aft.

Moxey glanced upward in the direction of the CCR and saw the connection team coming down the ladder from the manifold. They had just completed their job of connecting the terminal's chicksan arms to the vessel's pipelines. The twenty-man team streamed passed

51

the two seamen and she waited patiently as they paraded down the gangway, one by one.

Waiting for them to pass, she asked Bickle, "How are things on this ship?"

"I've been on better," Bickle replied with distaste.

"What's wrong with this ship?" she asked.

"The captain and the mate. A couple of hard noses. They just fired a guy."

"For what?"

"Going up to watch drunk."

"Sounds to me like they did the right thing," she said brightly.

Bickle snorted. "No breaks on this ship."

As soon as the last man had passed and the ladder was clear, she left her bags at the gangway with Bickle and proceeded up the ladder to the cargo control room.

■ ■ ■

The CCR was crowded with a dozen visitors and three Japanese interpreters. In the middle of the space was the cargo control console. The console consisted of two sides: a ballast side and a cargo control side. The complicated-looking battery of knobs, buttons, and indicators controlled the valves and pumps for the various tanks. Briscoe was facing the cargo control side, his eyes locked on the digital tank pressure readouts, while everyone else in the room watched him. He was not happy.

17.1 psia, the readout indicated.

Beside him was his control room partner, Brad Bensinger, the cargo engineer. Both men were edgy as they watched the tank pressure indicators. The pressures were increasing.

17.2 psia

In the background, the grinding sound of an old, dot matrix printer was heard. Second mate Mike Heyerdahl was running the printout for custody transfer. Custody transfer was the process of officially gauging the amount of cargo the ship was delivering to the utility company. All five cargo tanks were being measured for temperature, density, and level. It was important because this provided the figure that would be the basis for payment to the sellers. The gauging of the cargo was done electronically utilizing sensors in the tanks. Five printouts were run and then averaged together to derive the final measurements. The old printer was so sluggishly slow that each printout took over a half-minute to complete.

17.3 psia

As part of the operations procedure, the ship's tanks had to be "bottled up" with nothing flowing in or out of them during custody transfer. This was done in order to achieve stable readings from the tank's sensors. Any flow, liquid or gaseous, could affect the readouts. Due to the nature of the -265 degrees Fahrenheit cryogenic cargo constantly boiling off, the shore valve was always open when the ship was in port to relieve the tank pressures. During custody transfer this "bottling up" of the tanks meant that the shoreside gas valve had to be closed for a few minutes. This had always proven to be a difficult procedure to adhere to for the pressures in the tanks would rise.

Briscoe was having difficulty restraining himself with the two Japanese interpreters, Hiro-san and Yamaguchi-san, who were standing by. They all watched the rapidly climbing readouts. He could tell they were as nervous as he.

He looked over at the dot matrix printer, located across the room, and then at Heyerdahl who was operating the printer.

"Which printout is that?" Briscoe asked Heyerdahl.

"The third one, Jimmy. Two more to go," Heyerdahl replied.

Briscoe looked at the digital readouts.

17.4 psia

Briscoe never liked to play it too close when it came to the safety relief valve limits. When the safeties opened due to high tank pressure, cold, methane gas would escape into the air in the form of a white cloud. The white cloud, being heavier than air, would descend upon the ship until it warmed and expanded. By then the methane could possibly come into contact with an ignition source onboard or ashore and an unimaginable fire could result. He couldn't restrain himself anymore.

"Hiro-san, I can not wait until after custody transfer to open my shore valve. I have high tank pressures and I need to open it right away," Briscoe asserted.

"No, no, please wait until *after* custody transfer," Hiro-san said.

Briscoe shook his head in disbelief. "By that time my safety relief valves on the tops of the tanks will be lifting and we'll look like a five stack calliope as white vapor clouds blow into the air. Look at those readouts," he said firmly, pointing to LEDs on the console. "They're at 17.4 now! At 17.8 the safeties are going to slam open and we will all look very foolish. The whole cargo transfer operation will be delayed. We will all be busy sitting down at the conference table filling out forms explaining to Japanese port authorities why we lifted our safeties and spewed cold, combustible gas into the air!"

The two terminal reps said nothing.

After a long moment Briscoe asked, "Well, gentlemen, what are we going to do?"

The two Japanese terminal personnel looked at each other. Yamaguchi-san finally said, "I will talk to dock supervisor."

"Yes, you talk to 'dock supervisor,'" Briscoe said with some relief as the man walked over to the telephone. At last, he was making some headway. He glanced at the readouts. The pressures had risen to 17.5.

■ ■ ■

Greta Moxey entered the control room just then and looked around the crowded room for the chief mate. Behind the console she saw a good-looking man who seemed to be in charge talking to an uptight-looking Japanese fellow.

"I can't believe you won't give me permission to open my shore valve with my pressures so high," Briscoe complained to the terminal representative.

"I am sorry," apologized the man, "but shoreside not ready."

"I don't care if you are sorry," Briscoe said to the man. "Shoreside *should* be ready. They *said* they were ready before we started custody. You tell us to bottle up and run custody transfer, but then say you're not ready."

"I am sorry," the terminal person apologized again.

"Swell. You're sorry. Great."

A woman's voice broke his concentration. "Excuse me. Mate?"

"Yes, what is it?" Briscoe said snapping his head abruptly with annoyance, looking for the source of the interruption. He did a double take and his annoyance faded when his eyes landed on the face of the attractive woman standing before him. The first thing that caught his eye was her hair. It was stunning. Long and thick. A rich, rusty red in color. She wore round, black-framed designer glasses and the eyes behind them were bright and a soft gray. She was cheerfully dressed in a red and white jumper. She could have passed for either a graduate student or a young fashion industry executive.

"I'm the new AB."

"The new AB. Oh, yes. You're Greta. Greta...Moxey?"

"Yes, that's right."

"Good. Pleased to meet you," Briscoe said, momentarily at a loss for words. He found her beauty distracting. Greta Moxey the able-bodied seaman turned out to be a very lovely girl.

Third officer Paul Lindvall entered at that moment with the mail.

Moxey asked, "Which watch do I have, Mate?"

Lindvall said, "Here's the mail. Brad gets it all again."

He handed Bensinger his mail. The cargo engineer sat down for a moment and began leafing through the stack of letters.

Lindvall continued, "Jimmy, you only received a big package from the office, but it was too big to lug up here so I left it in your room."

Briscoe never took his eyes off Moxey. "Thanks, Paul."

"I'll be standing by the manifold if you need me," Lindvall said, and turned to leave.

"Fine," Briscoe said.

Greta Moxey waited patiently for a moment, but when the chief mate said nothing, she broke the silence and asked, again, "Which watch do I have, Mate?"

"The, ah...hmm, watch. Which watch *do* you have? That's a good question. Oh, yes, the four to eight watch." He chuckled over his own lapse and, embarrassed, gave himself a rap on the head with the palm of his hand. He said, "The four to eight. Forgive me, things are a bit confusing here as you can see," Briscoe said, sweeping his arm through the air.

He then felt very foolish indeed, for he knew he was acting like a bumbling fool at that point. Here he was, in charge of this huge ship and its operations, and he found himself tripping over his mouth, trying to apologize to a young, new AB who knew nothing at all about the operation at hand except that it's chief officer was obviously taken by her and had trouble speaking.

"The four to eight," she repeated pleasantly as she turned to leave. "Okay. Thank you."

"Yes. Head back to the house and see Captain Leech. He'll sign you on."

"Thank you," the girl smiled and headed for the door.

The terminal representative hung up the telephone and returned at that point.

"Okay, Mr. Mate," Yamaguchi-san began. There was suddenly grave concern in his voice. It was as if he had just been struck by a bolt of enlightenment. "Terminal said it is ready to accept your boil-off before completion of custody transfer. You may now open your shore valve."

Briscoe continued to stare after the new AB, almost mesmerized. To Yamaguchi-san, he said, "Thank you."

The readouts now showed 17.7 psia. The terminal people suddenly found themselves becoming agitated as Briscoe stood there doing nothing.

"Please, Chief Officer," Hiro-san said, urgency rising in his voice. "You may open your shore valve...now."

Bensinger looked up from leafing through his letters and wondered what was Briscoe's delay.

As she opened the door, rusty red-haired Greta Moxey glanced back at him and was surprised to find him still looking at her. She gave him a sort of puzzled yet pleasant, have-a-nice-day kind of smile and exited.

"Please, Chief Officer!" Hiro-san implored, almost to the point of begging.

"Huh...oh, yes. Very well," Briscoe finally said.

Without taking his eyes off the door, Briscoe slowly reached for a button in the center of the long, cargo control console and pressed it lightly with the tip of his finger. A shot of air blew through the system's manifold pneumatics and the large, sixteen-inch valve swung open.

"Gas valve open, Jimmy," Lindvall's voice crackled over the radio's speaker.

"Thank you," Briscoe answered into the radio.

The tank pressure readouts instantly began to drop to reasonable levels. The Japanese representatives breathed a sigh of relief.

Briscoe glanced at the door.

Bensinger noticed. "Jimmy, what did I just see here a moment ago?"

"What are you talking about, Brad?"

"Did I see what I thought I saw?"

Briscoe was confused. "What was that?"

Bensinger said, "Tell me that I didn't just see a 'smitten' chief mate."

"What?" Briscoe became annoyed. "No. *Nonsense.* What are you talking about? Go back to reading your letters."

Bensinger smiled. He knew what he had seen.

Briscoe shook his head. "Smitten. Ha!"

He didn't want to admit it, but he had just felt a slight breeze blow by his heart.

Chapter Seven

Southbound to Bontang

The next morning, the docking and harbor pilots came aboard, four tugs secured themselves to the ship's shell bitts, and the twelve, steel mooring wires were cast off. The huge tugs pulled the LNG carrier clear of the dock, turned it around, and then escorted her down Osaka Bay until she was clear of the navigation hazards that lurked in the area. The pilots then disembarked and the *Majestic Prince* sailed for the eastern coast of Borneo where the little equatorial town of Bontang was located. Bontang was one the loading ports for the GascoTrans fleet.

Briscoe sat in his office sifting through a pile of stores invoices and company operations letters the ship had received while in port.

"Big deal," he said to himself.

No letters from home.

But then why would there be?

After two, long months the lack of letters from home was beginning to bother him. Receiving letters from home was a part of pulling into a port. In addition to time ashore, it was what everyone onboard lived for. He had received them from Heather for more than ten years, and now there were none. He missed Heather's warm letters and found himself having trouble focusing on the company paperwork.

Katey froze...

He needed to get outside.

Sam stopped by his door just then with a telex in hand.

"Well, Jimmy, we're finally on our way. Southbound again," the short, stocky man said excitedly, rubbing his hands together. It was obvious the sixty-three year-old man was excited about seeing his twenty-one year-old girlfriend again.

"Oh, joy. Back to the jungles of Borneo," Briscoe said dryly, rising from his desk. Seeing the telex in the radio officer's hand, he asked, "Is that for me?"

"No, it's for the chief engineer. Nothing interesting. Just our sister ship, the *Endurance*, trying to track down spare electronics cards, is all. It seems they fried half the cards in their cargo console somehow during Typhoon Wendy."

"Yes, I heard they got tangled up with Wendy and suffered a lot of damage. Lost an anchor, too."

"I heard that's a wacky ship."

"Why's that?" Briscoe asked.

"They're always experiencing troubles. That's the one where the captain shot himself after they ran aground, right?"

"Yes. Unfortunately. He was depressed. His wife left him."

"Sounds wacky to me. I guess you have to be wacky to go to sea. I thought you knew that."

"Only sixty-three year-old radio officers who tinker around with teenage girls are wacky," Briscoe said as he headed for the door.

"See? I knew it. You're jealous, after all, Jimmy. I can tell."

"No, I'm not jealous," Briscoe scoffed. "I've got to get out of here. Check some things on deck," he said, leaving the office.

■　■　■

It was a beautiful day outside. Briscoe decided to shelve the office paperwork for the time being and spend his working day out on deck instead.

He walked down the four deck ladders within the house and stepped outside onto the main deck. Before the accident, he would have paused to take in the brilliant sunshine and the fresh, sea air. Before, it was moments like this one that made him think he was, indeed, a lucky man. He would think, "What executive in a crowded city, what laborer in a dingy factory, what sales clerk in a monotonous shopping mall, could step outside their workplace door and bask in the beauty and purity of nature?" How many times a day did these very people ashore suppress their Walter Mitty-ish daydreams of standing in his very own shoes, on the deck of a great ship out in the middle of a tranquil sea, free from all of their cares? And to be paid for it to boot! Before, it was moments like this one that made Jimmy Briscoe remember why he had chosen a seagoing career in the first place. There were no such moments now to ease his pain and loneliness. The absence of letters only reminded him of it.

He headed forward.

Along his route he walked passed cargo tank five. The cargo tanks on the Quincy-built, Aquarius-class LNG carriers employed the spherical tank design. Five gigantic, aluminum balls in a straight line; each 120-feet in diameter; the lower halves of the balls sat hidden deep below the main deck while the upper halves were covered by a layer of protective steel. These sky-reaching, half-spheres are what gave this type of LNG carrier its distinctive look. No other type of cargo ship in the world looked like this.

The cargo tank covers were in constant need of maintenance and that morning Briscoe found Bosun Knuckles supervising three sailors at tank five. Darryl Hawkins, Mo Silalahi, and his new AB, Greta Moxey. They were already making drops, repelling down the curved surface. Briscoe surveyed with satisfaction the safety lines Knuckles had in place and watched as the sailors worked their way down the tank. They were touching up places which had been recently chipped and primed, where cancerous-like rust had eaten its way through the paint coating and caused ugly, brownish stains to streak downward like tentacles all the way to the main deck. The sailors were carefully lowering themselves down the side of the tank domes. They were seated in bosun's chairs, paint rollers in hand, paint cans dangling between their legs from the hooks fastened to their safety belts. Bosun Knuckles had them out working immediately after departure. He wasted no time in "turning the people to" - i.e., putting them to work - and making the most out of the good weather while it lasted. Typhoon season was at its peak now in the Western Pacific with tropical depressions forming on a regular basis and both he and Briscoe wanted to get ahead of the inevitable lost workdays that were coming.

Briscoe was pleased to see that Darryl Hawkins had finally come around and was at last being an asset to the ship. His instincts about the man had been good. Darryl was reading the seaman's book he had loaned him and it seemed to be showing.

Standing next to cargo tank five on the main deck, Briscoe observed the deteriorating condition of one of the ship's large, three thousand pound dry chemical fire fighting units. He walked over to it for a closer inspection and noted the hose reel and the dry chemical tank were in good shape, but the unit's valves were badly rusted. He began working them and cakes of rust fell to the deck. As he manually opened and closed each valve, he glanced upward. Thirty feet above him, Greta Moxey was making a descent.

Briscoe noticed Moxey looked entirely different than when he had first met her in the CCR the day before. She was still pretty but the designer glasses were gone and the stunning, rusty red hair had been squirreled away into two insignificant, girlish pony tails which dangled happily from the back of her head. She was dressed in worn, green fatigues that seemed to have years of paint splattered on them and a loose-fitting, faded chambray shirt.

Moxey stopped, dipped her nine-inch roller into a partially filled five-gallon bucket, and eagerly began rolling out the creme-colored paint over the recently primed steel. Her eye caught Briscoe's just then and she broke into a smile.

"Good morning, Mate," she said pleasantly.

"Good morning," he answered in return, impressed. The girl was actually enjoying her work. There was a childish delight in her face, the expression of a person trying out a new experience for the first time. It was as though making a drop down the side of the tank was a new adventure for her. Briscoe couldn't remember ever having seen any of the male crewmembers working so hard, much less with smiles on their faces.

He returned to his inspection of the fire-fighting unit and walked around to the other side of it to check the condition. He hadn't been there for more than a minute when suddenly there was a dull thud followed by a scraping sound from high above. He instantly looked up and saw Moxey's five-gallon paint can sliding down the side of the dome. In an instant, the can slammed hard onto the main deck ten feet from where he stood and sent splattering lines of creme-colored paint streaking through the air. Briscoe was shielded from the paint splash by the dry chemical unit itself. The main deck, which was red in color, was now a blotched mess, as was the after side of the dry chemical unit.

"I'm so sorry," she said, stunned, with fearful uncertainty about what her new boss's reaction would be. Her first day on the job and she drops a half-filled, five-gallon can of paint on the chief mate. Some chief mates would have been screaming their bloody heads off by now. To her surprise - and relief - this one was not. She lowered herself down the side of the tank.

Bosun Knuckles hurried over to survey the damage. Knuckles, a patient, yet stoic man, was obviously embarrassed by the accident. He walked over to the scene and said wryly to the new AB, "Next time wait until he's *under* you before you try to hit him."

Briscoe was not upset. He said to Knuckles, "I don't know about our new AB, Bosun. She hasn't been here more than twenty-four hours and already she's trying to kill me."

"It wasn't my fault," she said innocently as she continued lowering herself to the main deck. "The line just broke."

Briscoe walked over to the spilled bucket and inspected the line. The ends of the line were chafed and frazzled.

"This stuff is looking pretty old, Bosun. Better replace all the lines with new so we don't have any more accidents."

"Yes, sir," Knuckles grumbled.

Moxey set foot on the main deck, climbed out of her bosun's chair, and unbuckled her safety harness. That was when Briscoe noticed her cotton work gloves. One was red, the other green.

"Cute gloves," he quipped, raising an eyebrow. "Except you have them on the wrong hands. The red one should be on your left hand and the green should be on your right." He was referring to location of the red and green navigation lights on a ship, which she was obviously trying to mimic.

"I always get them mixed up," she said gaily, and then produced a hearty laugh. She was relieved he wasn't angry. "You'd think after two years at sea I'd remember that by now."

"Where in the world did you find red and green cotton gloves?"

"In Osaka yesterday, while I was shopping. They come in packages of a dozen red and a dozen green. So I bought two packages and paired them myself."

She then proudly displayed her gloves by promptly rotating her hands outward like a magician showing an audience that his hands were empty.

"I see," he said. Briscoe then directed his attention to the parted line again. Surveying the mess on deck, he said, "It wasn't your fault. I'll let you get away with your attempt on my life this time. Bosun, let's get this mess cleaned up."

"Yes, sir. No good stuff," Knuckles growled. "I'll throw the entire coil in the incinerator, Mate. Moxey, go aft to the paint locker and grab yourself some cleanup rags and a can of thinner. Dell's back there stirring paint. Ask him to give you a hand."

"Yes, Bosun," she said with delight. The AB then gave Briscoe a radiant smile and left for the bosun's locker. She was happy she wasn't in any trouble.

"Sorry, Mate," Knuckles apologized.

"Don't worry about it, Bosun," Briscoe said as he watched the young girl go, her ponytails swaying back and forth. "Accidents do happen," he heard himself saying.

As she departed, Briscoe wondered how calm he would have remained had the AB been a man.

■ ■ ■

"F&B - 1520" was written on the crew dining room white board.

"Not another fire and boat drill," Clarke Bickle scoffed as he entered the crew dining room and saw the message scribbled in big, white chalk strokes on the chalkboard. It was coffee time and he was the first one in the deck department to break early.

Bickle was twenty-five years-old, a lanky five-foot-ten, and a clown with a drinking problem. He was above average in the brains department, but had never done anything with his brains other than go to sea and sail as an able-bodied seaman. Like so many young people, alcohol and drugs had zapped him of the motivation needed to go further in life. As a result he stagnated, took the route of least resistance, was unhappy with himself, and made up for his failure by being a wise guy.

Arnie Dell, also an AB, was right behind him. "What? Boat Drill? Oh, what a bummer, man. We just had one."

Dell had just turned thirty, but acted like he was nineteen. He was a man carefree and without responsibilities. His family owned a half-dozen ships and was well off. Being the only child, he knew someday he would inherit the family wealth. *Why bust buns when there was nothing to worry about?* was his attitude. As long as he shipped and proved to "Dear Old Dad" he could keep a job, he knew he had life knocked.

Bickle and Dell had just come in from chipping paint on the stern. The *Prince's* stern deck was covered with cakes of rust and they were using jet chisels to strip the deck down to bare steel. The work was slow and tiresome. Both men were covered from head to toe with dirt and rust. They took off their safety goggles and threw them down on one of the dining tables. Rings of soot remained around their eyes.

"God, I hate fire and boat drills," Bickle complained sourly as they walked over to the coffee pot and took a Styrofoam cup each. Bickle poured.

"Hey, man, are you kidding? Look at the bright side: we won't have to chip rust until after the drill. Our work day has been shortened by almost an hour," Dell noted happily as he took his cup and dropped his burly, two hundred pound frame squarely into a chair beside a dining table. His motto was "while at sea work as little as possible, and when at home don't work at all."

"Fuck that. I'd rather work than stand around and play games," Bickle whined.

"Yeah, I know you, Clarke, you lazy son-of-a-bitch. You hate the drills because you're afraid the chief mate will designate you 'the man in charge' and make you put out the phony fire," Dell said goading his friend. He laughed and added, "You're afraid you'll look foolish."

"I'm not afraid of looking anything," Bickle lied defensively. "I don't care. If the mate tells me to do it, I'll do it. I'm not afraid of any lousy simulation. He can pretend the whole fucking ship is on fire and if he assigns me to take the fire parties around to put out fires, I'll do it. I don't care. I can fight a fire as well as the next man."

Dell laughed. "Right. Who are you kidding? You don't even know where the nearest fire hose is."

"Fuck you, Arnie, you lazy asshole. I hope the mate picks *you*. In fact, I'm going to volunteer you. I'm going to say that 'Arnie Dell says there isn't anything he doesn't know about fighting a fire aboard ship.' He says 'everyone else doesn't know jack shit.'"

Dell sipped his coffee, laughed, and said loudly, "No, no. Don't say any of that or I'll volunteer *you!*"

Both men laughed as Bickle sat down across from Dell with his coffee.

"Hey, what do you think of that new AB?" Bickle asked. "Is she a looker or what? Catch that hot, red hair of her's."

Dell nonchalantly replied, "She's all right."

"Just 'all-right'? 'All-right' my butt! You'd jump her bones if you could, Arnie, and you know it."

"She's not *that* great looking. Like I said, she's okay. She made one helluva mess on deck today. I had to help her clean it up. Boy, did that suck," Dell complained.

"What happened?" Bickle asked.

"The securing line to her paint bucket let go and fell on deck. What a klutz. Who needs a girl on a ship?"

At that moment Moxey walked in with Darryl Hawkins and Mo Silalahi immediately behind her. They were coming from tank five.

Dell quickly put his hand to his mouth and snickered, wondering if the new AB had heard his big mouth comments. Apparently not, for she didn't seem offended.

Bickle merely looked at him and rolled his eyes. He then watched Moxey as she entered the room and walked to the coffee machine.

Dell blurted, "Darryl, I see you got the bosun to let you make a drop down the side of tank five."

Darryl poured his and Moxey's coffee and said, "Like they say, 'the squeaky wheel gets the grease.'"

"Getting logged, though, man," Dell said. "Was it worth it?"

"Yeah, what did old Stone Face Leech say about it?" Bickle chimed in.

Darryl sat down at the next table, coffee cup in hand. "Captain Stone Face, he say one more time for *anything* and I'm hist'ry."

Greta Moxey asked, "What is it you did?"

"I went down the side of the tank when I wasn't suppose to."

Bickle and Dell roared with laughter. Bickle said, "Darryl, tell her the rest of it."

"What happened?" she asked.

"He went down the side of the tank at night while drunk," Bickle said.

"You didn't," she said, surprised.

"I wasn't drunk. But I did go down the side of the tank at night," Darryl said with pride.

"What did the chief mate do?" she asked.

"He called me to his office and told me if I didn't get my shit together he'd fire me and pull my papers."

"Pull your papers?" Moxey asked, wondering what kind of man this chief mate was.

Bickle and Dell roared again with laughter.

"'Pull his papers!' He told you that?" Bickle asked.

"Sure did," Darryl admitted.

"And you believed him?"

"Is there any reason why I shouldn't? After all, he is the mate."

"He can't pull your papers, man," Dell said. "He's bullshitting you. Only the Coast Guard can do that."

"Whether he's bullshitting me or isn't doesn't matter," Darryl said, trying to hide his ignorance of such things. "He can still fire me."

"The chief mate seems like a nice enough guy," Greta said, curious about the man.

Bickle detected a note of interest in the girl's tone. Knowing of Chief Mate Briscoe's reputation for fairness and his own budding interest in this cute, rusty red-haired seaman, Bickle decided to shoot down the competition.

Bickle said, shaking his head, "Can't trust him. He's always trying to nail someone's ass to the wall."

"Yeah, he's a shmuck," Dell said, seizing the opportunity to slander the mate.

"That's not so," Mo Silalahi adamantly spoke up. "Chief Mate Briscoe is a fair man." Silalahi was the elder AB in the deck department, and Moxey's watch partner. A strong, compact man of fifty with a boyish face and black hair, he was loaded with more seagoing experience than most of the deck department combined.

"Fair? Look what he did to George," Bickle went on.

"George was drunk and couldn't stand his watch," Silalahi said. "That was the second time, too. He got what he deserved."

"I don't trust him," Bickle continued. "That chief mate doesn't like me. Never did. He always picks on me."

Silalahi said, "You don't do your job, Bick-o. That's why he picks on you. You do your job and he *won't* 'pick' on you."

Moxey asked, "Is he married?"

"Married? Yeah, he's married," Dell said throwing in his two cents worth. "He's also a regular playboy! He and his wife must not get along or some damn thing."

Bickle added, "Yeah, he's always playing with the hired help around here. Christ, they say he was shacked up with the last steward's assistant that just got off here for a month."

Silalahi shook his head. "You guys are nothing but a couple of liars. They're lying, Greta. Don't listen to a word they're saying."

"Am not. You'd better watch yourself, Greta," Dell said. "He might put the make on you next."

Moxey shrugged. "What guy out here *doesn't* try to put the make on me? He sounds normal."

"Well, you better watch yourself anyway. He might take away *your* overtime if you're not 'nice' to him," Bickle advised.

"You're full of it, Bick-o," Silalahi said with disdain. "Chief Mate Briscoe, he's a nice guy. Greta, ask anyone, except these two derelicts. Chief Mate Briscoe he don't mess with anyone." Silalahi got up to wash his cup and added, "You guys are full of shit."

Moxey was confused. She didn't know who was telling the truth; nor did she care. She was there to do her job and have some fun if she could. She wasn't there to get mixed up with personalities.

She said, "I can handle myself. I'm not worried about it. Like I said, he seems like a nice enough guy."

■ ■ ■

At 1520 the general alarm bells sounded and the crew gathered in the main deck passageway for the weekly fire and boat drill.

Clarke Bickle stood beside Moxey while second mate Mike Heyerdahl took a muster. Every crewmember's name was called out. Just then he saw the chief mate coming down the narrow passageway.

"Hey, Mate, why don't we have a Martian Invasion Drill?" Bickle asked with sarcasm, trying to impress the new AB with his wit, as Briscoe walked by him.

Briscoe ignored Bickle's wry comment as he always did and continued on his way toward the front of the group.

"What's a Martian Invasion Drill?" Moxey asked.

"Oh, nothing. It was just something I read in a book once about a bunch of crazy, foreign flag sailors," Bickle replied.

While crewmembers continued to pour into the main deck passageway and line up in their appropriate squads, Briscoe said, "Bickle, come here a minute."

Bickle rolled his eyes. He muttered to Moxey, "Shit. See? I knew it. I knew he was going to pick me."

The lanky AB sauntered over to Briscoe.

"Yes, Mate?"

Briscoe took him aside. Speaking quietly so the other crewmembers could not hear, he said, "I want you to be the 'body' during today's fire simulation. Go up to the vacant cadet's room on the 03 level, lay out on the deck, and play dead."

"Is that all?" Bickle asked.

"Isn't that enough? You think you can handle that?" Briscoe asked.

"Yes, sir," Bickle replied, more than happy to oblige.

"And stay 'dead' until after the fire party has pulled you out. Okay?"

"Will do, Mate." Bickle then left through the weather door and went up the outside ladder.

Moxey saw Bickle being sent away and thought it strange. She wondered if he was being punished for something.

Briscoe then turned to Heyerdahl and asked, "Is everyone here?"

"Yes. Everyone's present," the second mate reported.

Briscoe then addressed the group. "All right. Everyone, listen up. Today we're going to have a simulation fire. I will designate one of you to be in charge of putting it out."

"Where's the fire going to be?" someone asked.

"They'll announce it over the PA," Briscoe said. "As always, take charge. Don't be afraid to use the equipment, and don't be afraid to grab the people you need to help you extinguish the fire. Any questions?"

There was silence as Briscoe looked at each and every face. No one had any questions. They never did. Trying to get people interested in the fire and boat drills was like trying to coax high schoolers to read Shakespeare. Simulations were the only way to get their attention.

"No questions? Okay, then," Briscoe shrugged. "Everybody knows everything, as usual. Here we go."

Briscoe then looked directly at Moxey and said, "Greta, you will be in charge of fighting the fire today."

Greta blinked, surprised at first. She hadn't expected to be called upon so soon after boarding the ship.

Briscoe called the bridge on his radio. "Bridge-Chief Mate. Okay, Paul. Make the announcement."

A moment later third mate Lindvall's voice boomed over the PA. "Attention on board...Fire on the 03 deck! Fire on the 03 deck!"

Moxey quickly sprang into action. She organized her squad with impressive speed. She assigned AB Silalahi and OS Hawkins to don self-contained breathing apparatus and then led the rest of her squad up to the 03 deck.

While Moxey and her group used the interior stairway, Briscoe went up to the 03 deck via the outside ladders. He arrived before the fire party and assumed a position just out of view where he could watch what was going on.

When Moxey and her squad arrived they were surprised to find actual smoke billowing out from underneath the cadet room's door.

"Oh, my gosh!" she said, stunned. "It's a real fire!"

Simulations were simulations. Crewmembers go in and fight a *make-believe* fire. Real fires were never set aboard ship just for the sake of practice. Moxey was incredulous as that thought flashed through her mind. She wondered, did they actually set a real fire for this drill? That's crazy! Maybe it's a real fire that just *happened* to coincide with the fire drill.

Whatever the case may be, she pointed to the 03 deck fire locker and ordered, "You two men run the hose from that fire station."

The two men instantly obeyed. To another gawking seaman, she said, "You...get a fog applicator and put it on the nozzle."

The gawking seaman grabbed the fog applicator that was stored in the same fire station as the hose and attached it.

Just then Silalahi and Hawkins arrived wearing the breathing apparatus. Their air tanks were strapped to their backs, their masks were snug against their faces, and their air valves were turned on. Their breathing through the units' regulators made them sound like Darth Vader with a respiratory ailment.

69

"Take this fire hose and prepare to go into the cadet's room," Moxey said to them.

The two men who had stretched the hose out handed the nozzle to Silalahi while Hawkins grabbed the hose. One man ran back to open the valve and charge the hose. Silalahi and Hawkins then began to advance toward the cadet's room. Smoke continued to pour out of the room at an alarming rate.

"Give me water," Moxey shouted to the man standing by the valve at the fire station.

The man instantly turned the valve and the one-and-a-half-inch hose filled and stiffened under the one hundred pounds of water pressure.

At this point Briscoe appeared in the passageway. "Hold it!"

Moxey and the rest of the squad all turned their heads.

"Listen to me: you people are doing good so far, but don't open that nozzle. I don't want water all over the place."

"What?" someone asked.

"What about the fire?" someone else asked.

"Don't use the water," Briscoe repeated. "Keep your hose charged, but do not open that nozzle. Okay, continue."

"Son of a gun! I'll be damned," Darryl said. "There ain't no real fire in there."

"Okay, nozzle man, open the door," Moxey said to Silalahi."

Silalahi bent low and turned the doorknob. More smoke billowed out, but the AB noticed one thing was missing: heat. He shoved the door and it swung open all the way. He and Hawkins then began to advance into the smoky space, dragging the water-charged hose in with them. Visibility was almost zero in the cadet's room. As a result of Briscoe's order not to use water, the two sailors knew there was no fire. Once inside they heard what sounded like a small motor noise coming from the corner. They were about to investigate when Silalahi glanced down on the deck and, through the smoke, saw something else.

"Casualty! Casualty!" he called back to Moxey.

"Where?" Hawkins shouted.

"Right there!" Silalahi shouted back. "On the deck in front of you!"

Moxey heard the shouting from within. She yelled, "Bring him out!" To the others in the passageway, she said, "It must be Bickle. He was sent away by the mate during the muster." Turning to one of the other squad members she said, "Go down and get that basket stretcher we passed in the main deck passageway."

The man nodded and hurried away.

Silalahi and Hawkins appeared just then backing out of the cadet's room carrying Bickle.

"Where do you want him?" Silalahi asked as he emerged from the room.

"Set him down right here and then go back into the room and find the source of the smoke," Moxey directed.

They set the AB down on the deck and went back into the smoky room.

To two other men, she said, "Move Bickle to the end of the passageway where he won't be in the way."

Just then the crewman returned with the basket stretcher.

"Wait a minute. Place him in the stretcher first," she said.

The men lifted Bickle, placed him in the stretcher, and were about to move him when Silalahi and Hawkins reappeared. They were carrying an odd-looking device no bigger than a small kerosene heater. It was making a sputtering sound and smoke was shooting out of a holed exhaust pipe on the device's side.

"What the devil is that thing?" Dell asked.

"A smoke generator," Moxey said with a smile.

"That's what it is," Briscoe said stepping forward. He took the machine from Silalahi and flicked a switch on the unit's side. The machine went dead. "We just received it in Osaka. I thought I'd test it today. It seems to work just fine. You all did real well, and Greta, you did a good job being in charge."

Moxey smiled proudly.

"Hey," Bickle said, still lying on the stretcher, "isn't Greta going to give me mouth-to-mouth resuscitation?"

"Why would she want to do that?" Dell asked. "She doesn't want to catch any diseases."

"Hey, watch it scar face," Bickle retorted.

"Sorry," Briscoe said, "you didn't make it, Bickle. You were in the smoke too long."

"You dead, man," Hawkins said. "Feed him to the fish."

"Some shipmate you are," Bickle replied as he stood up.

"Oh, well, man. That's life," Hawkins responded with indifference.

Dell looked at Hawkins standing there in his air pack and facemask. "You look like the 'brother from outer space' in that get-up, Darryl."

"Hey, man, whatever it takes," Hawkins replied. "Just doing my job."

Briscoe said, "All right, everyone break down the equipment and put everything away." He then spoke into his radio. "Bridge-Chief Mate. The 'fire' is out and we'll be ready for abandon ship drill in a couple of minutes."

"Standing by," third mate Lindvall's voice crackled over the speaker.

■ ■ ■

At the end of the long workday Briscoe jogged up the port side of the ship to the gym for his daily workout. He was dressed in shorts and a body shirt. The gym was located near the bow of the great ship, in the forward stores space just below the main deck. The forward stores space was originally designed for storage, but because it was so vast and the overhead so high that, over the years, it had been adapted for recreational purposes. In addition to being a place to keep the weight-lifting equipment, it was also used as a half-basketball court. The space's after bulkhead also served as a backboard for both racquetball and tennis. To make the sports activities and workouts more enjoyable, the crew had pooled their money and had outfitted the space with a stereo system.

As Briscoe entered the forward space and walked down the ladder he heard music coming from the stereo. Halfway down the ladder he saw a couple of crewmembers playing one-on-one basketball. He then saw Greta Moxey. Gone were the baggy, green fatigues and the green and red cotton gloves. She was now dressed in a Spandex exercise outfit and was off to the side of the basketball court doing an aerobic dance routine. Gloria Estefan's *The Rhythm is Going to Get You* was playing.

Moxey saw him coming down the ladder. She smiled and said, "Hello, Mate."

"Hi," he said, and walked over to the weight lifting equipment on the port side, only a short distance away.

Briscoe noted that Greta Moxey looked very good in tight Spandex. With current fashions as they were and the baggy look being in, he hadn't noticed her figure when he had first met her in the CCR or out on deck where she was dressed in her work clothes. In the Spandex exercise outfit, however, she had a very nice figure.

Briscoe also noted she was an excellent dancer. Her body was alive and full of energy as she danced her way around the basketball court. Her rhythmic moves radiated excitement. They were fluid and precise, yet carefree and natural. She was driven by the music. She and the *Miami Sound Machine* were one, and that made her fun to watch.

"How long have you been doing aerobics?" he asked as he began placing weights on the Olympic bar.

She looked up and answered, "Since high school."

"You dance well."

"Thanks," she said with a bright smile. "I love aerobic dancing. I'm able to keep fit and listen to good music at the same time."

Just then the song ended, the tape was over, and the boom box shut itself off. Moxey stopped dancing and walked to the stereo to flip the tape over. Briscoe finished loading the Olympic bar with two hundred and fifty pounds.

"You did pretty good at the fire drill today," he said as he lay down on the bench and prepared to press.

Moxey skipped the stereo for the moment and walked over to him instead.

"Good? I did great!" she asserted with enthusiasm. "I enjoyed that. I like the way you run your drills, Mate. None of the other ships I've been on do simulations at their drills. It was fun being in charge."

Briscoe exhaled and pushed the heavy bar off the uprights.

"Most guys don't like to be in charge," he said. "They're afraid they'll make a mistake and look foolish. They forget the drills are for practice. But you jumped right in there and got the people moving."

He began pressing the weight.

"I almost panicked when I arrived on the 03 deck and saw the smoke," she laughed. "I thought the fire was real."

After six presses Briscoe returned the weight to the uprights.

"That was my curve ball for the day. But you handled it fine."

"Thanks," she said with a warm, self-assured smile. "The smoke was a good idea."

Briscoe rose from the bench and began placing more plates on the Olympic bar.

Moxey was suddenly concerned with the large amount of weight Briscoe was adding to the bar.

"That's a lot of weight, Mate, to be starting off with without a good warm-up," she cautioned.

"This *is* my warm-up. I can handle it," he said confidently.

"Oh?"

Briscoe lay down on the bench again and prepared to press.

"How did you become involved in shipping?" he asked.

"A friend of mine from high school ships out and she told me all about it. About the sea, the ports, the money, the interesting people out here. I thought 'That sounds neat! That's the life for me!' What a great way to see the world."

"Are you going to make a career out of *this*?" he asked with a slightly jaded tone.

"I'd like to. I'm studying for my mate's license now and plan to have it in three years. After that, who knows? Depending on the job market, maybe I'll eventually work my way up to captain."

"Good luck. The job market isn't that good," Briscoe said as he began pressing again, "and it's only going to get worse."

"When are you going to have your master's license, Mate?"

"I've had it for years," he answered while he pressed the weight upward.

"And you're *still* sailing chief mate?" she asked with scrutiny.

The pointed question caught Briscoe off-guard and irritated him. It caused him to lose his concentration right in the middle of the press and he could no longer push up the weight. The heavy bar slowly came down on him and pinned him to the bench. Moxey saw he was in trouble and quickly hurried around to the back of the bench. She grabbed a hold of the bar and gave him the additional lift he needed to get it up.

"Push, push, push!" she said with encouragement.

He lifted the bar with her help and they placed it on the uprights.

"Good work, Chief Mate," Moxey said happily. "That's too much weight, though."

"Thanks," he said as he took in a breath of air. Returning to her question he defensively answered, "The industry is dying, the American flag is disappearing from the world's oceans, and there's hardly any advancement anywhere. If you look at the license rack you'll see it's *full* of master's licenses. Where are you from?"

"Annapolis. I'm camping out at my folks' house, playing the 'old maid.' Where do you call home, Mate?"

"Up in Vermont. South of Burlington in a little town called Pristine."

"It sounds like a cold place to be."

"It is. But it's a beautiful place to be. Plenty of mountains, skiing, lakes. The four seasons. I just love it. It's a great place to raise kids."

"Oh. How many do you have?"

Gilly...Katey...

He hesitated at first, and then said, "Two. A boy and a girl. Four and three."

"That's great," she said. "Do they remember you when you return after four months at sea?"

"Oh, sure. They always remember."

"That's good. Well," she said, suddenly glancing at her watch, "time to finish my routine before watch." She headed for the stereo to flip over her tape.

"Me, too," Briscoe said, as he began removing the excess plates from the Olympic bar.

A moment later *The Miami Sound Machine* filled the space with music and Moxey began dancing again. She then asked, "Do you workout every day, Mate?"

"Almost. I have a six-day on, one-day off routine."

"Wow. That's a lot. If you keep working out like that they'll cast you for *Terminator IV* instead of what's his name. I'll see you down here every day then. If you ever need a spotter, yell out."

"Okay. Thanks."

"Any time," she said with a smile. She then continued her aerobic routine while Briscoe prepared to press again.

"By the way, Mate, if you were the sun, what time would you set tonight?"

"What?" he asked, puzzled.

"I have to be on the bow at sunset. What time will the sun set?"

"Oh...about six-thirty."

75

"Okay. Thanks," she said, and danced on.

Briscoe watched her for a few moments before pressing weights again. There was something very different, something very pleasant and delightful about this young lady. He still couldn't put his finger on it, but whatever it was it left him with another warm feeling.

■ ■ ■

As the days went on and the *Majestic Prince* continued on her southbound journey to Borneo, Briscoe observed that Greta Moxey was becoming an asset to the ship. The young AB worked with relentless energy and constant good cheer. Bosun Knuckles - a typical, old-fashioned, women-on-ships-hater - quickly grew to like her when she impressed him with her painting and cutting-in ability.

She operated the ship's jet chisels - a device like a miniature jack hammer - with aggression and chipped greater areas of deck scale than any of her male shipmates. She pulled heavy mooring lines and slushed, or greased, wires with the men. She loaded and hauled stores when needed. She was prompt at relieving the watch and was an excellent lookout who never missed anything that appeared on the horizon. She could steer the huge ship as well as anyone on board.

One day, Moxey and her shipmates chipped and wire-brushed the deck around the swimming pool, and then they painted the entire area with rollers. Briscoe walked by and took a moment to observe the progress. Bosun Knuckles was supervising.

Briscoe asked, "How's the new AB working out, Bosun?"

"She is fast and neat, Mate," Knuckles replied with satisfaction. "I've never seen anyone work as hard as that girl."

One of her duties as AB was the daily cleaning of the bridge. Every morning she'd polish and shine, and sweep and swab, and then empty the trash. The *Prince's* bridge had never seen such care. She took a special interest in the bridge and every day she had a new question for either Briscoe or the second mate.

Never wanting to be late for bow lookout, she would call the bridge every afternoon and ask pleasantly, "Mate, if you were the sun, what time would you set?"

Moxey was proving herself to be a hard worker and no one in the deck department could complain otherwise. She was rarely moody - if she was, she hid it well - and continuously energetic. She got along with everyone and most everyone liked her. Unknowingly, Greta Moxey was beginning to motivate her male co-workers and Briscoe noticed the productivity of the deck department increased. Even Dell and Bickle picked up their languid pace a little, and never realized it.

Chapter Eight

Bontang, Borneo

The *Majestic Prince* arrived in Bontang, Kalimantan eight days after departing Osaka.

Located on the island of Borneo, Kalimantan is part of Indonesia and is the largest of the three divisions that make up the huge island. The island is also home to the sultanate of Brunei and a part of Malaysia. Borneo has the distinction of being the third-largest island in the world, and is located on the western Pacific Ocean southwest of the Philippines in the Malay Archipelago between the Sulu and Java seas.

The port of Bontang is situated four miles north of the equator on the eastern side of Kalimantan, along the Makassar Strait. At one time Bontang was merely a tiny, nondescript, fishing village at the edge of the thick jungle. When the natural gas fields to the west were discovered, it was determined that the fishing village had the best location to build a port from which to transport the valuable resource. Jungle lands were carved away, a shipping channel was dredged, port facilities created, a small airport was built, and a liquefaction plant erected. An extensive compound to house the hundreds of incoming ex-pats to build and operate the plant was constructed, stores and shops popped up, and where transient people and sailors went, brothels and massage parlors soon followed. The first shipment of liquefied natural gas left Bontang for Japan in 1977 aboard the American vessel *LNG Aquarius*. As the years went by, satellite dishes began sprouting up on the thatched roofs of ramshackle houses. Bontang can now be found in a world atlas, though, most of its inhabitants are still poor and rarely see any of the benefits of the government-run, natural gas exportation project that sits in their backyard.

When the *Majestic Prince* arrived that morning, an Indonesian pilot boarded and took the ship up the narrow Bontang Channel. At the head of the channel lie several of the liquefaction plant's huge, white storage tanks, and the three docks. Beyond that lie palm trees as far as the eye could see. A short time later the vessel was positioned alongside the dock by three tugboats, the eyes of the mooring wires were passed over the dockside hooks, and the ship was secured alongside the loading platform.

■ ■ ■

Briscoe and Brad Bensinger stood outside the CCR, monitoring the Indonesians connecting up the loading arms to the ship's manifold. While they waited for the workers to finish, they saw a number of crewmembers going down the gangway. Briscoe noted Moxey was among the shore-goers.

"Here we go again, Brad. The crew gets to go off and play while we're stuck on the ship," Briscoe said, wishing he could go, too.

"It doesn't seem fair, does it, Jimmy? But that's what we're paid the big bucks for," Bensinger said. The cargo engineer then noticed Moxey going down the gangway. "Your new AB is going ashore, too. She's one good-looking girl, man."

"Yes, she is," he agreed.

"Why don't you ask her out?"

"I can't do that, Brad. I'm her supervisor. Besides, I don't want to."

"Whatever you say, Jimmy," Bensinger said, not believing him.

Sam stopped by at that moment on his way ashore.

"What'cha up to, Sam?" Briscoe asked.

"Not much. I'm going ashore to see my new girl and take her to the house I rented last month."

"You've got a house here now?" Bensinger asked. He always kept up on the exploits of Sam-the-radio-man. The house was a new twist.

"Yes, sir," Sam answered. "Complete with maids and servants."

"How much does that run you?"

"Not much. Sixty, seventy bucks a month."

"Wow!" Bensinger exclaimed, truly surprised.

"Yes, you can live like a king over here," Sam added happily as he glanced in the direction of the jitney which had just pulled up. "Well, time to go, Gents. I just stopped by to see if you fellows wanted anything from shore."

"No, Sam. Thank you," Briscoe said.

"Brad?"

"Yeah, I'd like a young girl about twenty, maybe five-foot-four, and one hundred and ten pounds," Bensinger said jokingly. "Think you could manage that request, Sam?"

"I'm sure I'm could, but I don't think I'd get her very far past plant security," Sam answered.

"Oh, well. Never mind then."

"See you two later," Sam said, and then he headed for the gangway.

When Sam was out of earshot, Bensinger said, "Sam, the 'sixty-year-old stud.' He's something else. I wonder if he really *does* anything over there besides talk about it?"

"Whatever he's doing here, it's keeping him young," Briscoe said.

Briscoe watched as Sam and the others walked down the ladders to the dock and then boarded the company jitney. A moment later the jitney was rumbling off down the dusty road for town.

"You had your turn ashore, Jimmy," Bensinger said. "Remember, you were a third mate once and you used to go off all of the time."

"Yeah, I know," Briscoe said with disappointment. "With age comes responsibility."

"Hey, I just remembered. According to the schedule we'll have a day or two at anchor next time. We'll be able to go off then - that's if old 'Leechy Baby' will let you. We can go off and have a beer."

Briscoe's blue eyes brightened. "Yeah, that's right. I forgot about that. Hmm. Good idea." There was restrained excitement in his tone.

Briscoe turned and went back into the CCR, leaving a puzzled Bensinger behind.

"What's so special about having a beer?" Bensinger wondered to himself.

■ ■ ■

There were two places a sailor or an ex-pat could go for entertainment while ashore in Bontang. One was known as the Prakla, or the massage and brothel district. The Prakla was situated entirely on a rickety, wooden pier that ran several hundred feet long and had dozens of cheap bar/massage parlors on both sides. All anyone had to do was walk down the middle of the pier, dodge a wandering chicken or two, and decide whether to go left or to go right. The rest was all the same: the warm beer (there was no ice), the throbbing disco music, and the rows of tiny rooms where the young girls lived and massages were performed. It was a filthy place and when the tide was out the smell of raw sewage seeped up between the rotting floorboards. After a bunch of beers, however, none of that mattered to the patrons; especially once the sun had set and the lights were dimmed. People didn't come to the Prakla to read *Popular Science*.

The other place a sailor or ex-pat could go - the only decent place outside of the Prakla to dance and eat - was the Indi Hotel lounge. The Indi's main building was a plain, single level, prefab concrete structure that housed the register's office, the restaurant, and the dance floor. Upon entering, the dance floor was immediately on the left while the dining room was off to the right, adjacent to the bar. Beside the bar, a walkway with a small courtyard led to a second building out back where the hotel rooms were located.

The jitney pulled up to the Indi and Greta Moxey was the first to jump out. Followed by Steward Stancy, chief cook Fritz Sonnenschmidt, and two of the steward's assistants, she went inside. Loud disco music played over the dance floor speakers. The place wasn't packed with people yet, but there was a respectable turnout for dinner. Darryl Hawkins and a pretty, Indonesian girl were the only ones dancing. Moxey and the group found a table close to the dance floor, sat down, and ordered drinks. Looking around the spacious dining room, Moxey saw Clarke Bickle and Arnie Dell eating in the far corner, and Bosun Knuckles was also there, having dinner by himself several tables away. In addition, there were several Indonesian patrons.

A small Indonesian fellow appeared with a bottle of beer in his hand and he stepped into the tiny glassed-in booth.

"The DJ's back," Moxey said to the group.

He flicked on a handful of switches, jammed a cassette into one of two players, and suddenly another song - a Madonna disco-mix - erupted through the four large speakers that hung in each corner.

"Come on," Moxey said to Clarence. "Let's dance."

"No, I'm gonna have a drink first, Greta. I'll dance with you after Fritz. Fritz, you dance first."

"My pleasure," the ebullient, rotund cook said.

Greta took turns dancing with them all. She danced with Steward Stancy and, again, with chief cook Sonnenschmidt. She danced with the two steward's assistants, Juan and the new guy, Jack. Fritz Sonnenschmidt was the best dancer of the bunch. Despite his orb-like physique and three hundred and forty pounds, his moves were smooth and, like any good dancer, he let the music flow through him. He was also the only one who could keep up with her. The others tired quickly like old men and were forced to sit down.

Bickle and Dell watched the dance floor activities with little interest from the far corner while they finished their seafood dinners. Their table was lined with a dozen empty beer bottles; partial evidence of an all day binge. First, they had gone to the Prakla where they each had a traditional Asian sandwich - i.e., sex with two girls - and then to the Indi for dinner and further refreshments. Both men were feeling no pain.

After watching Moxey out on the dance floor, Bickle decided he wanted to dance. He stood up unsteadily from the table and bumped into it, causing the empty bottles to rattle.

"Where ya goin'?" Dell asked.

"I'm going to dance with Greta."

"Dance? You can't even stand fucking up!"

"No problem, man. I can stand."

"Right," Dell scoffed as he guzzled his beer.

Even though he knew his good buddy Dell was right, Bickle headed for the dance floor. The song ended just then and Greta had just sat down. He walked up to her and said hello.

"Hi, Clarke," she said, returning his greeting.

Bickle attempted to look sober and politely asked, "Greta, would you care to dance?"

Greta noticed he was unsteady, his eyes had that tired, glazed look, and that his breath stunk of alcohol.

"No, thanks, Clarke," she smiled. "Maybe next time."

"I know...you think I'm too wasted to dance," he said slurring his words.

Greta couldn't think of anything else to say but, "Yes!"

Just then the DJ put on another platter. The speakers began pumping ear-deafening rhythms again.

"I'm really okay, Greta," Bickle said raising his voice to be heard above the throbbing sound.

"No, you're not," she declared loudly. Some other time, Clarke." She then turned to Fritz and said, "Come on, Sonnenschmidt. Another dance."

"Absolutely," Fritz agreed and he leaped out of his chair.

Fritz and Greta flew out onto the dance floor, leaving a blurry-eyed and pride-hurt Clarke Bickle behind. He went back to his table and plopped himself down into his seat.

"Well, 'Fred Astaire,'" chided Dell. "What happened to your dance?"

Bickle stared out at the dance floor at Moxey and the cook. "Ah, she's a bitch."

Dell then said, "Watch me, Casanova. I'll dance with her." He pushed his chair back, making a lot of noise, and stood up.

Sitting three tables away, Bosun Knuckles looked up from his dinner when he heard Dell push his chair. He watched as the sailor made his way to the dance floor.

Dell tapped Sonnenschmidt on the shoulder and said, "Excuse me, Fat Boy, I'm cutting in."

Hawkins heard Dell and didn't like what he said.

"Huh?" the cook said, surprised by the interruption.

Dell then tried taking Moxey's arm, but she pulled it away.

"No, thanks," Moxey said sternly, shaking her head.

"Hey, man. What are you doing?" Hawkins asked.

"I'm dancing with Greta," Dell said.

"No, you're not, Arnie. You're as wasted as Clarke," Moxey said. "Go back to your table and leave Fritz and I alone."

"Yeah. Leave her alone, man," Hawkins said, attempting to block Dell.

Dell shoved Darryl across his foot and the ordinary fell down on the dance floor.

"Oh, 'sorry,'" Dell said insincerely.

Hawkins angrily got up and was about to strike him.

Moxey quickly said, "Don't do it, Darryl."

Hawkins hesitated.

Dell ignored Hawkins and focused on Moxey. "Oh, come on, Greta. I'm a much better dancer than sphere-man here," he said, slurring his words.

Just then someone tapped him on the shoulder and said, "Dell."

Dell turned around. Bosun Knuckles stood a foot away.

"What's up, Bosun? You want a dance?"

"No, I don't. I want you to go back to your seat and quit bothering people."

"All I want to do is to dance with Greta."

"You heard her. She doesn't want to dance with you, so go back to your seat and leave her alone."

"I will when I'm ready," Dell sneered. "I'm ashore now. I don't have to listen to you, *Bosun*." Dell emphasized the word "Bosun" by jabbing his index finger in Knuckles' chest.

Before Dell had pulled his finger away, Knuckles had grabbed his hand and twisted it backwards at the wrist, forcing Dell to drop to his knees.

"Ahhh!" Dell moaned.

Knuckles looked down at the man and said, "Now, listen, Dell. If you're going to cause trouble, I'll have the owner of this place, who happens to be a dear friend of mine, call the police and take you away to jail. Ever spend the night in a Bontang jail? I can guarantee you won't be out in time to make the sailing in the morning. Now, are you going to be a good boy and apologize to these fine people?"

"Yeah, okay, Bosun," Dell said.

Knuckles released him. Dell staggered to his feet and rubbed his sore wrist. He reluctantly looked at the chief cook, Moxey, and Hawkins and said, "Ah, sorry."

Fritz acknowledged the apology by saying, "No problem."

Greta nodded her acceptance, adding, "Yeah. No harm done."

Hawkins said nothing.

Dell then sauntered back to his table.

"Thanks, Bosun," Greta said to Knuckles.

"Yes, thank you, Bosun," Fritz said.

"Sometimes the only thing these guys need is a little *guidance*," Knuckles said with a smile. He then headed back to his table to finish his dinner.

Returning to his table, Dell said to Bickle, "Come on, man. We're not getting anywhere with that bitch. Women on ships. What a bunch of crap that is, huh? She's not going to dance with us so let's quit wasting time here and go back to the Prakla. I want to get another lube job before I go back to the ship."

"What the hell. Sounds good. Let's go," Bickle agreed.

The two rose from their table and they headed back to the Prakla.

Shortly after they had left, Sam Waerhauser came in with his new girlfriend. He saw Greta on the dance floor and waved.

"Sam, do you want to dance?" Greta asked.

Surprised and flattered, Sam sat his girlfriend down, quickly explained to her that Moxey was a shipmate and not another girlfriend, and then went out onto the floor.

Greta Moxey was having the time of her life. She danced and danced. She danced with anyone who was able to keep up with her. No one could. Even Fritz Sonnenschmidt finally pooped out by the end of the night. Her energy was boundless.

■　■　■

The next day the wires were let go and the ship left the steamy, jungle port behind, heading for Japan with her 125,000 cubic meters of cryogenic cargo. Briscoe had received word of the Arnie Dell incident from Bosun Knuckles that morning and decided to hold a meeting in his office to discuss it. Knuckles, Bickle, Dell, Moxey, and Hawkins arrived.

Dell showed up with a tape recorder.

"Do you mind if I record this meeting?" he asked.

Annoyed, Briscoe answered, "Yes, I do. Turn that silly thing off. What do you think this is? *Law & Order?* Trying to build a case for an attorney?"

"Well, no," Dell lied.

"Here, give it to me and I'll set it on my desk," Briscoe said curtly, holding out his hand. Dell reluctantly handed him the device. "Pick it up when we're done."

When all were present, Briscoe said, "Everyone take a seat. This won't take long."

Everyone sat down and the chief mate began. "All right. I was disappointed to hear about the incident that occurred last night at the Indi Hotel. I appreciate Bosun Knuckles bringing it to my attention and I respect his desire to handle it in his own way. Since no one is filing a complaint with me about it, I'm not going to get involved any further than what I'm going to say to you here and now."

Bickle raised his hand. "Mate, can I say something about last night?"

"No. Don't want to hear it. I don't want to hear from anybody. I'm not going to ask each of you for your take on what happened. I got a clear enough picture from the bosun. Now, Mr. Dell and Mr. Bickle, I do wish to make it clear that any further incidents like this will not be tolerated. If I ever hear of this type of conduct again, then some heads will roll and you two will be fired."

"Fire us? For what?" Dell asked, his tone indignant. "I didn't lay a hand on her. Besides, you don't have any jurisdiction ashore, Mate."

A regular sea lawyer, Briscoe thought.

"You're right about that, Mr. Dell. I don't. But sexual harassment and making a ship unseaworthy does fall within my jurisdiction."

"Sexual harassment? Unseaworthy? What the devil are you talking about, Mate?" Dell asked. "How does what happen ashore make this ship 'unseaworthy'? We didn't do anything to the ship."

Briscoe said, "A ship's seaworthiness extends beyond just the simple 'equipment failure' or a 'crack in the hull.' It also includes the condition of the personnel onboard and the working environment that exists. If you two clowns create a hostile work environment for others aboard ship by your actions ashore, then you are creating an unseaworthy condition and it won't be tolerated. Don't think for one second that just because you're ashore, that you can get away with anything you want without consequences onboard. I won't waste one moment cleaning this situation up if it happens again. Consider this your first and last warning."

"I don't believe this," Dell muttered.

"Well, believe it," Briscoe said becoming increasingly annoyed with the man's tone. "You may find *this* hard to believe, Dell, but we - everyone onboard - have to get along. We're on a ship together and anything can happen out here at sea at any time. We need to be a team. You may not like each other, but at some point, maybe not today or tomorrow, maybe not this year, but we have to be able to depend on each other because you never know when we may have to save each other's lives. Now I want you two to do a better job handling your drinking and behave yourselves when you're ashore. If you don't, then you leave me no choice but to have Captain Leech fire you. Are we all on the same page now?"

No one said anything.

"Dell? Bickle?" Briscoe asked, looking directly at both seamen.

Both men grumbled what sounded like a "Yes, sir."

"All right. Then we're done. Meeting's over. Back to work."

Everyone filed out of the room and Briscoe returned to his desk and paperwork. A minute later there was a knock on his door. Briscoe looked up. It was Bickle.

"Back already? Didn't you just leave?" Briscoe asked.

"Yes, Mate."

"What's up?" Briscoe asked, though he could guess by the quiet and embarrassed expression on Bickle's face what the man wanted.

"Mate...can I have a tube of Blue Gel? I woke up this morning and found crabs."

Briscoe looked up in disbelief at the man. "Did you fool around again in the Prakla last night?"

Embarrassment sweeping across his face, Bickle said, "Well, I don't think it's any of your concern-"

"In other words, you did. I don't understand guys like you, Bickle. You're still on the erythromycin the doctor prescribed after your last visit to the Prakla two weeks ago, right?"

"Yes, sir."

"The doctor gives you a shot of trobicin in the right cheek, puts you on erythromycin, and tells you to come back in four weeks for tests. You know you've got a case of the drip and yet you have no idea what it may be. It could be a small urinary infection or it could be gonorrhea. But you *still* head over to the Prakla, fool around with the girls, and spread it around."

"I know. I guess it doesn't make sense," Bickle said, and then happily added as an afterthought, "but, hey, I'm not dripping anymore."

Briscoe shook his head in resignation. "Well, that's makes everything okay then, huh?"

"Sometimes I don't think straight when I'm drinking," Bickle admitted.

"Did you ever think, Bickle, maybe you shouldn't drink?"

"Yes, but then sometimes I overdo it."

Briscoe shook his head with resignation. "Meet me at the ship's hospital at coffee time and I'll give you the Blue Gel."

"Thank you, Mate," the seaman said and left.

As soon as Bickle had left his office, Sam knocked on his door. He had a telex in his hand.

"Yes, Sam?"

"Manetti, the steward's assistant, and Hobson, the wiper, are due to be relieved next time in Japan," the radio officer said, handing him the slip of paper.

"I'm sure they'll be happy to hear that," Briscoe said, unconcerned. He tossed the message in the "Incoming" tray on the corner of his desk. "Sam, the only telex I'm interested in is the one about *my* relief."

"I hear ya. You're a lucky guy, Jimmy. Being home for the holidays and all."

"Yeah, swell. The holidays."

All alone. Can't wait.

"Can't wait," he said blandly. He then realized how fast the year was passing. The last holiday home he had lost his family.

"I'm sorry, Jimmy," Sam said, realizing that was when the tragedy occurred. "I didn't mean to...I mean, I forgot, that's all. I only meant that...well, you'll be home for the holidays. I *love* the holidays, and I wish you the best and that you find happiness."

"I know what you meant, Sam. Don't knock yourself out stumbling over words. Thank you for the well-wishing. I appreciate it. So, tell me about this new girl of yours," Briscoe said, trying to change the subject.

Sam said, "She's a pretty girl. A real, nice girl. She's twenty-one. I bought her contract from the mamasan and freed her from the slavery of the Prakla. Now she's living at my house where it's clean and she can have almost anything she wants."

"That's quite benevolent of you, but, Sam - and I don't want to sound cynical - but isn't she just going from one form of slavery to another? Sort of like a cold room maid for your rented house?" Briscoe asked, playing the devil's advocate.

"What do you mean?"

Briscoe was blunt. "Why don't you give her a plane ticket home and let her return to her family?"

"She *wants* to stay in Bontang, Jimmy," the radio officer said defensively. "I'm not making her do anything she doesn't want to. I gave her a bank account. She's free to go at any time. Although, I may marry her."

"Get out of here, Sam," Briscoe scoffed. "You've been talking about marrying one of these girls for years and you still haven't done it yet."

"Oh, but this one is different. I never liked a girl enough to buy a girl's contract before."

"Well, invite me to the wedding," Briscoe said dryly as he dove back into his paperwork.

"We stopped by the Indi," Sam said. "That new AB of yours was there."

Briscoe leafed through his papers. "Yeah. I heard."

"Boy, is she quite the dancer. She was dancing with everyone. She even danced with me. You like to dance, don't you, Jimmy? Too bad you have to be here on the ship during cargo operations. You'd have a blast with her."

"Yes, it is a shame," Briscoe said with feigned sadness.

Little did the radio officer know, the upcoming anchor time during the next trip to Bontang was shaping up as the foremost thing on Briscoe's mind.

No cargo ops at anchor meant shore time for the chief mate.

■ ■ ■

The northbound trip to Japan was a busy one for the crew. With a typhoon far ahead of them to the north, viciously slamming Japan, the weather was superb where the ship was located, and ideal for outdoor maintenance work. The crew continued to work hard, and with an uncanny sense of fun. Briscoe found Moxey possessed the nature of an impish little sister at times, playing harmless tricks on shipmates. One day while washing down the *Majestic Prince's* deck with a fire hose, she sprayed Dirk Mainline, the Herculean first engineer, as he was out for his daily jog. Mainline wore dreadlocks and they were a matted down mess after Moxey had showered him with seawater. Mainline didn't mind. On another day, Briscoe spotted her and a couple of the ABs briefly playing "Star Wars" with the pneumatic jet chisels. They were pretending to zap each other while they worked and the jet chisels rattled in their hands. By the end of the hot day, under the scorching tropical sun, more chipping had been accomplished than Bosun Knuckles had seen in a long time.

There was one afternoon the crew was slushing the stern mooring wires and their supply of grease ran out. The grease was stored in the storeroom on the bow and a couple of the ABs took a four-wheeled cart and headed forward to fetch more. Briscoe was walking aft when he saw them approaching. He laughed when he saw Moxey sitting on the empty cart being pushed ahead by two, burly seamen. She sat with her arms crossed, looking like an Egyptian queen being transported by her slaves.

Moxey continued to perform well at the fire drills, being an able follower when others were given the duty of being in charge. Even at the drills she had moments of levity with the crew. During Briscoe's lecture on CPR, she posed for a picture of herself standing with her arm around the propped-up rescusi-Charlie training doll. Moxey and the doll looked like old chums.

The crew was working so hard during the voyage that Captain Leech granted Briscoe's request and held a pool party to reward them for their efforts.

On the afternoon of the pool party the weather was perfect - clear sky, calm sea, and little wind. Steward Stancy and Fritz, the cook, set up a spectacular supper feast on one of the picnic tables on the pool deck. Captain Leech supplied a few cases of beer and soda from the ship's slop chest. Mahoney, the new steward's assistant, brought his boom box out to the party and there was music to dance to afterwards. It wasn't long before someone asked Moxey to dance and she gladly did. As the pool party went on into the early evening, most everyone, except Dell and Bickle, took turns dancing with her. Few could keep up with her. At one point she was dancing with Fritz. Fritz was a fabulous dancer and Moxey's favorite dance partner. Fritz decided to be innovative during one dance and he suddenly abandoned Moxey and ran to his room. When he returned he had an enormous hoola-hoop in his hand. He dropped it over his head, down to his ninety-inch waistline, and then continued dancing with her while twirling the hoop around his rotund belly.

Briscoe watched and laughed, but kept his distance.

Moxey continued to appear in the ship's gym daily, doing her aerobic exercise and practicing her dance steps. After the pool party her passion for dancing was known throughout the ship and she found herself holding a group class for a half-dozen shipmates who had asked for instruction. She began holding class in the evening after watch. Briscoe noticed during the trip that she stopped wearing her Spandex exercise outfit. Instead, she wore baggy gym shorts and a T-shirt. He thought, perhaps, she was becoming more aware of how her Spandex displayed her fine figure and the need to be more conservatively dressed, particularly in front of a group of male, seagoing dance students.

Every time Briscoe saw her, whether it was during the day when she was working or in the evening when she was dancing or teaching the group, there was a twinkle in her eye at all times. It didn't matter whether she was patiently instructing one of the hopelessly clumsy fellows in a new dance step or outside in the drizzly, miserable rain performing a mundane, uninspiring chore such as washing down the deck or hauling trash. Greta Moxey was enthusiastic about everything and took pleasure in all that surrounded her. The ship, the people, everything in life.

She seemed to approach her day with the radiant enthusiasm of a youngster with a brand new toy - and Briscoe found this characteristic irresistibly attractive.

Chapter Nine

A Step Forward

Arrival day came and the *Majestic Prince* docked at the Osaka Gas Terminal.

The busy day flew by for all hands and as the evening hours passed, the discharge of the liquefied gas cargo proceeded smoothly. All was quiet in the cargo control room. Bensinger had gone aft for a break and Briscoe sat alone, his eyes surveying the bank of digital readouts that monitored the ballasting operation and the movement of the 125,000 cubic meters of liquefied natural gas from ship to shore.

The door to the CCR opened just then and Briscoe looked up, expecting to see Bensinger. He did a double take when he saw Greta Moxey enter. She was an entirely different-looking woman than the one he had been seeing on deck every day. She was dressed to kill and had just returned from the action of the Osaka nightclubs. Her designer glasses were gone, replaced by contacts. Her rich, rusty red hair was spectacular, thick and flowing; just like the day when she first came aboard.

"Your hair is stunning!" Briscoe said with enthusiasm. They were the first words out of his mouth.

"Well, thank you!" she said, happily, surprised by the compliment.

She was carrying a small shopping bag as she approached him.

"What are you doing?" he asked.

"I just returned from Osaka. Whew! What a great time I had dancing. The clubs are so lively here and the people are so friendly. I brought you something, Chief Mate."

Moxey reached into the shopping bag, produced two bags of potato chips, and set them down on the desk beside him.

Briscoe laughed and said, "Potato chips?"

"At the pool party I heard you asking the Steward if he could order some different types of chips and he said he couldn't. So, there you go. One is barbecue, the other is salt and vinegar flavored."

"Well, thank you, Greta. You didn't have to do that."

"You're welcome. I have to keep my chief mate happy and if all it takes are chips, then I'll buy you chips. Besides, I owe you after nearly dropping that bucket of paint on your head."

"So...that *had been* intentional," he said, ribbing her.

"Of course not!" she responded defensively.

"Well, I don't know if I'm that easily pacified. I'll tell you what: I'll let you off the hook under one condition."

"And what might that be, Chief Mate?" she asked with suspicion.

"We're going to be anchored in Borneo for a couple of days. I'll be free of cargo duties and I'll be able to go ashore. Would you like to have dinner with me?"

"Dinner? I don't know," she said with sudden caution.

Her eyes looked away from his for a moment and the radiance in her face flickered. She obviously had been taken by surprise. A moment later the radiance reappeared.

She smiled, and said happily, "We'll see."

Briscoe instantly realized he had crossed the line. "That's okay. Bad idea. Don't worry about it," he said, dismissing the invitation. "I'm sorry. I shouldn't have asked."

"All right, then, Mate. We'll go out on a 'date.'"

"You don't have to, Greta. It's okay. Really. I guess I'm just not myself tonight. It's late," he said, glancing at his watch.

Moxey studied him seriously for a moment. "I appreciate you asking, Mate, but...you are the *Mate.* Now, I don't mind taking a ribbing from the rest of the guys about going ashore with the Mate, but I don't want to look like a fool either."

"Why would you look like a fool?" he asked.

"Well, because you're *married*, that's why," she said pointedly, as if it should be obvious to him.

He nodded. "Yes...I understand. It's only a dinner, Greta, and it *is* in public. Anyway, as far as dinner goes, we don't have to eat together. I'm going ashore because I haven't had a chance to in years."

Moxey smiled and then nodded. "Okay. I feel better about this 'date' now."

"You'll go?"

"Sure. Why not?" she consented.

"Good."

■ ■ ■

A week later the *Majestic Prince* dropped anchor three miles off the Borneo shoreline to await her berth. A contained, yet excited Jimmy Briscoe was not the least bit displeased. It was his first date in years, though he cautioned himself not to get too excited or, at least, *appear* too excited about it. He knew it was more like a "quasi date" and was, basically, just going ashore to have dinner with a shipmate.

The gangway was extended down to the waterline forty feet below. Eight crewmembers, including Briscoe and Moxey, boarded the launch after the workday ended. Most were planning to spend the night ashore. The ride to shore from the anchorage took nearly an hour aboard the slow-moving craft. The launch wasn't really a launch. It was a workboat designed to handle the mooring lines of the LNG carriers. It couldn't travel any more than five knots in calm water and there were few places to sit onboard. While everyone else stood around on the boat's stern during the ride, Briscoe and Moxey climbed up on top of the cabin where the life raft was stowed. The life raft served as a comfortable seat and the fresh sea air blew through their hair. They arrived at the pier near the liquefaction plant and from there a company jitney was waiting to carry them to town.

■ ■ ■

Traveling along the dirt road to town, their jitney suddenly came to a halt behind what appeared to be a traffic jam in the middle of the jungle. Several cars and motorcycles were stopped and there was a group of Indonesians gathered in the road in front of the line of vehicles.

"What's going on?" Briscoe asked the driver.

When the driver said he didn't know, Briscoe and the others climbed out of the jitney and went to see what was the trouble. The people gathered were all looking with fascination at something in the road. Working their way to the front of the group, Briscoe and his shipmates were stunned when their eyes fell on the amazing site. A large, constrictor snake, twenty-eight feet long, was slowly crossing the road. It reminded Briscoe of being at a railroad crossing, waiting for a freight train to pass. No one dared to drive over it. It was an awesome creature who seemed totally oblivious to all of the humans standing there and watching it from a safe distance.

Once the snake had cleared the road and disappeared into the jungle, the drivers returned to their vehicles and continued on their way. The incident served as a reminder to Briscoe that there were still some things the influx of big money and technology into this region had not changed. The jungle was still the jungle.

A short time later they arrived at the Indi Hotel. "A run down, third world, single-story hotel; the best hotel that the little town of Bontang had to offer." That would be the best way for a travel brochure to describe the aging establishment. Briscoe noted little had changed since the last time he had set foot in the dimly lit place, years ago, when he was a junior deck officer.

The Indonesian DJ sat in his glassed-in booth and disco music was bursting from the speakers. However, the dance floor was empty and people were eating. Briscoe and Moxey sat at a table near the dance floor, reviewed the menu, and gave their order to the waitress.

"What was your scariest moment at sea?" Briscoe asked, after the waitress had left.

"Oh...that would be during my first trip as AB," Moxey said with a knowing smile.

"What happened?"

"We had just finished docking in Tobata and were letting go of the tugboat. The tug line had a messenger bent onto it and we had it on the winch drum so we could lower the tug line down to him."

Briscoe nodded.

"Well, the tug started to run for some stupid reason and the line took a huge strain. The guy tending the messenger panicked and let it go. The line just shot off the drum like a bullet, whipped around a set of bitts like that giant snake, and the end of the line grabbed my hand!"

"Oh, God."

"Yeah. It nearly pulled my arm out of its socket, Mate. It jerked me down to the deck and an instant later I found myself being dragged. I thought for sure I was going through the roller chock and over the side."

Briscoe cringed. "What did you do?"

"Fortunately, I was wearing my gloves and the line took the glove off my hand before I slammed into the chock."

"Whew! You were lucky. How badly were you hurt?"

"Not too bad. I was bruised up some, but nothing was broken. My arm took about six weeks to recover."

"Wow, what a lucky lady. Were you wearing your trusty 'ole red and green gloves?"

Greta smiled. "Yeah, I was wearing my trusty 'ole, red and green gloves." She paused for a moment and then asked, "What about you, Mate? What was your scariest moment?"

"My scariest moment...hmm. My scariest moment occurred on the *Prince* seven years ago when I was second mate. We were passing through the Singapore Straits. Captain Leech had the conn and I was the mate on watch. Just as we were passing through the narrowest part of the Straits, we lost the plant. We had no propulsion or steering, and ahead of us lie the shallows, less than a mile away."

"So what did you do?"

"Leech looked at me and before he even opened his mouth I had grabbed my radio and was gone. I flew down the stairs and made a three-hundred yard dash up the main deck in about a minute."

"Wow!"

"During the race to the bow, all I kept telling myself was 'Drop the hook before she grounds!' Once on the bow, I let go the port anchor, bounced it off the bottom, and then paid it out slowly so the dragging anchor wouldn't snap the chain. Finally, the ship began to slow. By then, the bosun and others had arrived and we did the same thing with the starboard anchor. We managed to stop the ship within two-hundred feet of going aground."

"Close one."

"Yeah. It was close all right."

"So, you're a hero. Is that when they made you chief mate?"

Briscoe nodded. "It wasn't too long after."

"Is that the only time you were scared?"

"Yeah. That was it." He then added sarcastically, "After eleven years of going to sea and being cooped up within the confines of a ship, the only thing that scares me now is I think I'm suffering from 'limited reality syndrome.'"

Great laughed and asked, "Don't you have fun out here, Mate?"

He shrugged. "Fun? Once in a blue moon, I suppose. Every day is practically a photocopy of yesterday."

"Gee, that's too bad you feel that way. You have to do what makes you happy, Mate. If you don't make yourself happy, who else will?"

"Is that Moxey philosophy?"

"It's common sense. Personally, I like going to sea. There's so much to do and see when you travel to these far, out-of-the-way places. We're so lucky. We get to visit places that we'd never ever think about traveling to. That's what makes going to sea interesting."

"I can remember feeling like that at one time," he said reflectively. "I guess I've had too many years at it." He then looked beyond her and saw Sam entering. "There's Sam. I'll be darned. He really does have a girlfriend here."

"She's young, too," Greta noted with mild surprise.

"That's Sam for you. This place is his fountain of youth."

Sam and his twenty-one year-old Indonesian girlfriend sat down at the next table. The girl was attractive and petite. Her long, jet black hair reached down the back of her brightly colored dress. Her face was fresh and pleasant. Being escorted arm in arm by wrinkle-faced, gray-haired Sam, who was old enough to be her grandfather, the couple looked terribly mismatched.

Greta said loudly, "Now, there's a guy who knows how to have a good time. How are you doing, Sam?"

"Hi Greta. Hi Jimmy," Sam said with the exuberance of an excited teenager. This is Zahara."

Briscoe and Greta greeted the young woman.

"Hello," Zahara said.

"Greta, would you like a dance later?"

"Sure, Sam. But I have to dance with the Mate first."

"Oh, I get it," Sam said. "Rank has its privileges, right, Jimmy?"

"No, Sam. Go ahead," Briscoe said.

"Rank has nothing to do with it," Greta joked. "He threatened to cut my overtime if I didn't!"

Briscoe winked at Sam and said, "Well, actually, Sam, she's on overtime right now."

"I knew being chief mate had its advantages, but I didn't know what they were until now," Sam said.

"These 'Mates,' I'll tell you, Sam. I can't wait until I'm a mate someday. I'm going to make it a policy of mine not to harass the male sailors on my watch."

"They'll hate you for it, Greta," Briscoe said. "Didn't you know? Men loved to be harassed by women."

Just then there was a loud, retching sound from across the room. It was followed by the sound of a chair falling over as an Indonesian man at a far table stood up with both his hands grasping his throat. Greta jumped up from her seat and dashed over to help. Briscoe quickly followed.

The man was no longer retching, but was still clutching his throat and Greta knew instantly he was choking. She came up from behind him, wrapped her arms around his mid-section, and began thrusting her fist into the man's abdominal region. In her attempt to give the man the Heimlich maneuver, the man's wife and friends were appalled and thought she was hurting him. The wife shot to her feet and, along with others, they tried to pull Greta off the choking man. Greta hung on, nonetheless, and continued giving the man the Heimlich maneuver.

Briscoe attempted to get the people away from Greta and calm them down, but had little success. One angry Indonesian punched Briscoe in the jaw.

"Son of a b-!" Briscoe cursed.

The angry man took another swing at him, but Briscoe blocked it and shoved him across the room where he lost his balance and slammed into a tray-carrying waitress. The waitress screamed and the serving tray she was carrying flew through the air and crashed to the floor. The man then landed on Briscoe and Greta's table, destroying it.

Sam decided to get into the act. He said to his girlfriend, "Zahara, tell those people that Greta is trying to save his life!"

Zahara then joined in the imbroglio, but had about as much success as Briscoe. People were too busy trying to pry Greta off the man.

Despite the chaos around her, Greta continued the Heimlich maneuver and with one, strong thrust, a piece of meat that had been lodged in the man's throat flew across the table. The man wheezed and coughed as he caught his breath. Soon, the crowd that had turned their wrath on Greta, realized she had saved the man's life. The man's wife was in tears as she apologized and thanked Greta. Greta warmly accepted.

Greta and Briscoe returned to their table only to find the waitress cleaning up its remains. Their dinner was scattered all over the floor as well. It had been on the serving tray the waitress was carrying when the Indonesian had crashed into her.

Briscoe and Greta looked at their table and the mess on the floor.

"Well, that was our dinner," he said.

They looked at each other and broke out laughing.

"Would you like to dance while they bring us another?" Briscoe asked.

Greta nodded and happily said, "Sure."

As they headed out to the dance floor, Briscoe noticed Arnie Dell and Clarke Bickle appear at the door. They had just arrived and were looking around to see who was there. When they saw Briscoe, they said something to each other, turned around, and then left. Moxey noticed them, too.

"Well, I guess you frightened them away," she said.

He was doubtful. "Those two have been awfully quiet since our 'meeting of the minds' last trip. Hmm. Maybe the talk did help. Oh, well," Briscoe said, and led Greta out onto the dance floor.

The music pulsated and they danced fast and hard. They danced for nearly an hour, stopped for dinner, and then returned to the dance floor for more. During a rare, slow dance Briscoe placed his arms around Greta. They had the floor to themselves. Gradually, he brought her close to him and held her tight. He stroked her hair and gently began rubbing her back. He gently put his lips to her long hair and blew into it as they made slow turns about the dance floor. She didn't seem to mind. When she looked up at him, he tried to kiss her. She turned her head away.

"Keep your mind on your dancing, Mate," she gently scolded him.

■ ■ ■

At eleven-thirty they headed back to the ship. They were the only ones returning and, aside from the boat driver, they had the boat to themselves. Everyone else was spending the night ashore and would be returning on the morning boat. Briscoe and Greta rode on top of the cabin again, sitting on the boat's life raft. They gazed up at the clear, starry sky overhead, admiring the constellations. The sea had kicked up and spray was coming over the bow. Ahead in the distance was the brightly lit *Majestic Prince,* it's huge, sodium vapor lamps illuminating the entire deck and house for miles.

Greta's eyes twinkled as she looked skyward. "That was a fun 'date,' Mate. Plenty of action. Plenty of dancing. Plenty of good food. A great night all around."

"You even got to be a heroine," he observed.

"That's right. I did. In that case, I'd say it was a *very* good date," she said, reassessing the evening.

"The pleasure was all mine, Greta. We'll have to do it again sometime."

Greta's twinkling eyes wandered for a moment. "Mate, I have to be honest with you. I don't like going out with married men."

Briscoe experienced a moment of regret. "Greta, if it was the kiss, I'm sorry. I shouldn't have done that. It just seemed like the right thing to do at the time."

"That's okay, Mate. I'm not upset. If anything, I'm frustrated. You're very nice and I really enjoyed myself tonight. I just don't want to get involved."

"Who said anything about getting involved?"

"Come on, Mate. Geez. There are times when I say to myself 'so what if a guy's married? Just go out and have some fun.' Well, I've had my share of grief doing that. Now, all I want to do is find the 'ideal man'; a man who is good-looking, warm, and caring. And *available.*"

"I doubt you'll ever find him at sea. Most of the guys out here are either crazy, married, or have marital problems and should be avoided at all costs."

"Thanks, Mate, for the encouragement."

"Don't worry, Greta. He's in the world someplace. He may be harder to find, but when a rare gem is looking for another rare gem, it will take longer. In the meantime, you do have to protect your heart."

"Well, I'm surprised, Mate. I didn't know you were the resident expert on such matters."

"Hey, I'm chief mate and I'm supposed to know everything."

"What would your wife say if she knew you were on a 'date,' Mate?"

Should I tell her the truth?

"She probably wouldn't like it," he answered.

"Of course not. She's probably home waiting for you, taking care of the kids, and is very lonely."

Should I tell her it isn't so?

She probably wouldn't believe you.

"I don't know," Briscoe said, guilt in his tone as he looked away from her. "Perhaps."

"Never say anything detrimental about a woman because no matter how far away she is, she'll hear it," she warned. "That's Coglin's Law from *Cocktail.*"

"I like that: a defender of the gender. How noble."

"That's why I don't want to go out with you again."

"Why did you go with me tonight?"

"I wasn't a hundred percent sure if you were lonely and looking for romance, or just out to have some fun ashore."

"And you're sure now?"

Greta nodded. "Without a doubt. I know you like me, Mate. I've known that since day one in the CCR when you went gaga over me in front of all of those people."

"I didn't go 'gaga' over you," Briscoe said defensively.

Greta laughed. "Oh, yes, you sure did. You were stammering and trying to be nice and looking goofy - all at the same time. It was pretty comical."

"I did not! I was distracted by the cargo operation."

"Right, Mate," Greta said, relenting. "Whatever you say. Mate, you're a nice guy. It's a shame you're married."

Tell her now!

I don't know how.

I don't want her sympathy.

"Yeah, I suppose it is," was all he said.

"I think I probably could fall for you, too. But..." She shrugged and then laid down on the life raft. She then added with a smile, "Thanks for caring about me, though."

"You're welcome," Briscoe said. "It's part of my job description to keep the crew happy."

Greta laughed and said, "Wake me when we're home, please?"

"Sure."

Greta then closed her eyes and tried to nap. A night out with the Mate or not, she still had the four to eight a.m. watch.

As the little boat chugged along toward the *Majestic Prince,* more waves broke over the bow, showering them with a light spray. Briscoe looked down at Greta and smiled again. Her eyes were closed and she looked so peaceful and pretty as she slept. She was an uncommon woman of beauty and strength; a woman whose delightful radiance he wanted to bask in. He yearned for her and was warmed by her presence...but he knew he couldn't have her. It wasn't right...or the time wasn't.

More spray flew over the bow.

Chapter Ten

_____

Angela

Looking down at the ocean from a position miles above the earth, one could see nothing but the dark, swirling eye of a typhoon, its large, thick, sweeping tentacles reaching out in all directions for hundreds of miles.

Descending through the cloud cover and breaking through it, one hundred and ninety miles to the north of the swirling eye, one could see the speck. In the vastness of the body of water it was the only speck to be seen for hundreds of square miles. It was all alone and insignificant, miniscule and defenseless against the forces of nature. Descending further, the speck took the shape of a ship, and then the name on the bow became visible. In big white letters, it read "SS MAJESTIC PRINCE." The sea broke over its enormous bow and the heavy sea spray flew aft the entire nine hundred and thirty-six foot length of the ship until it struck the bridge windows. The liquefied gas carrier *SS Majestic Prince* was hove to.

To hove to in the South China Sea. That was Captain Leech's order of the day. To protect his ship and crew. This would delay their arrival at the loading port of Arun in the northwestern tip of Sumatra, however, it was always better to arrive late than not at all.

More tropical cyclones develop in the western North Pacific than anywhere else in the world, with the storms first forming as tropical depressions to the east of the Philippines and moving westward across the Pacific to the Philippines, Japan, China and Vietnam. Based on long-term studies of the movements of tropical cyclones, a storm forming in August could be expected to travel in one of three directions. One historical track shows that a storm will move northwest and then swing, or recurve, to the northeast, narrowly missing Japan. The second historical track shows it will move northwest and then swing to the west-northwest, pass north of Taiwan, and then into China. The third track shows it zipping straight across the Philippine mainland where the land drains it of its force and then into the South China Sea where it would re-gather its strength. This last case scenario proved true for Typhoon Angela.

Angela had slammed into the Philippines with incredible force and velocity, flew over the mountainous Philippine terrain, devastated Manila, and left hundreds dead and homeless in her wake. It then shot out into the South China Sea and was still going full force.

The *Majestic Prince* was three days out of Osaka heading into the South China Sea when Angela suddenly began to act as if she had a mind of her own and deviate from the historical tracks. Instead of continuing westward toward Vietnam, the killer storm decided to park herself in the middle of the South China Sea, three hundred miles due west of Manila. This was due to a fast moving, unusually high pressure cell to the north. This great wall of high pressure acted as a barrier and blocked Angela from going anywhere. Angela sat and waited, her intensity building, the seas around her churning and growing. The longer she remained in one place, the more time she had to hammer away at the seas and build them.

Even at a distance of nearly two hundred miles from the storm's center the ship was falling prey to Angela's ferocity. It was already pitching and rolling moderately. To hove to - i.e., to turn the ship into the sea and proceed at the slowest of speeds to provide steerage - was the only practical - and safe - thing to do.

The mates spent their watches monitoring both the swell and wind directions, waiting for the wind to veer or to back. This would indicate the storm was finally moving in one direction or another. They kept an eye on the wind speed as well. An increase in speed *without* a change in direction could mean the storm was heading straight for them.

Nobody liked being in or near a typhoon. Standing bridge or engine watch in one was nothing more than hanging on to the railing by the forward bridge windows or hanging on to a railing in the engine room and endlessly shifting one's weight back and forth between the legs each time the ship rolled. Over time it was tiring.

Eating in the dining room was like trying to eat on a roller coaster. With each roll, plates and silverware flew off tables and crashed to the tiled floor while food splattered onto the bulkhead or landed in someone else's lap.

Briscoe did not work his crew on deck during those days, other than for general resecuring of the vessel. The ship rocked and rolled, up to as much as twenty-five degrees at times. Most of the crew sat in their rooms or lay in their bunks reading or watching television. Workouts in the ship's gym were impossible.

Sleeping at night was also impossible. This was especially true on the *Majestic Prince's* 03 and 04 decks which were further away from the vessel's center of gravity. The 04 deck was one hundred and five feet above the waterline while the 03 deck was nine feet below the 04 deck. On those decks the rolling actually *catapulted* anything that wasn't tied down, including crewmembers. In addition to being thrown out of bed, people just couldn't sleep because of the "crashing in the night" sounds caused when the ship rolled just a degree or so further than the previous roll and things, otherwise thought to be well secured, would suddenly break loose and crash to the deck or smash into a bulkhead. The noises reverberated throughout the steel house, creating ominous sounds, giving one the frightening impression that the ship was on the verge of breaking up. Some of the less experienced crewmembers slept with their life jackets, using them for pillows, just in case.

The unchanging wind speed and direction, as well as Sam's updated weather reports received from both Japanese and Filipino radio stations indicated it was a standoff between Angela and the *Prince.* The storm continued to remain stationary, waiting for the high pressure to the north to move eastward. Angela sat patiently like an automobile at a railroad crossing, waiting for some slow-moving locomotive to pass.

Captain Leech was becoming edgy as the hours slipped by and the delay increased. He was cold and impersonal towards his officers and crew, yet he was a cautious man. Briscoe respected him for this. He knew Leech was not one of the foolish breed of men who would say "Damn the weather! The schedule comes first!" and then push his ship full speed ahead into a raging storm and heavy swells, and into oblivion. A vessel's size in this type of weather provided no immunity against disaster. Huge ships have had their backs broken in weather such as this and disappeared without a trace. Despite Leech's edginess, he was not to be swayed from his lifelong conviction of safety first for ship and crew.

His conviction swayed, however, the next evening.

■ ■ ■

It was on second mate Mike Heyerdahl's four to eight p.m. watch that it happened.

Heyerdahl was behind the chart table looking at the wind direction and speed indicators. More sea spray from the bow hit the large, bridge windows.

"Damn. It's getting worse," he muttered to himself as he watched the needles on the indicators bounce around in the fifty to sixty knot vicinity. The wind howled as it blew over the house.

Heyerdahl hadn't been on watch for more than fifteen minutes when a nervous-sounding voice crackled over the VHF's speaker.

Standing by the window and keeping a lookout while Heyerdahl was at work behind the chart table, AB Max Hillert barely heard the voice over the wind noise outside. He walked over to the VHF to listen.

"Mayday! Mayday! This is Stellar Polaris. This is Stellar Polaris. Does anyone read me? Over."

"Second mate, come here. Quick!" Hillert called out.

"What is it?" Heyerdahl asked.

"Mayday! Mayday! This is Stellar Polaris. Come in."

"I heard someone say 'Mayday.'"

Heyerdahl stepped around the chart table and went to the VHF.

"Mayday! Mayday! This is Stellar Polaris. This is Stellar Polaris. Does anyone read me? Over."

Heyerdahl quickly picked up the VHF's handset and responded.

"Stellar Polaris, this is Majestic Prince. I hear you, but not very well. Do you read me? Over."

"Majestic Prince, I read you. I am freighter, Panamanian registry. We are adrift and taking on water. Require immediate assistance. Our position is latitude 16 degrees 25 minutes north, longitude 115 degrees 15 minutes east. Over."

Heyerdahl grabbed a pencil and copied down the position. He read it back to the caller to insure its accuracy. The caller confirmed it. He then quickly plotted it and then called Captain Leech.

Leech groggily answered his telephone. "Hello?"

"Captain, we have a Mayday. A sinking freighter about one hundred and fourteen miles away."

"All right. I'll be right up," Leech said. "Call Mr. Bris-coe."

"Yes, sir."

■ ■ ■

A few minutes later Captain Leech arrived on the bridge in his bathrobe and walked into the chart room.

"He's right here, Captain; about one hundred and fourteen miles south-southwest of us," Heyerdahl said, pointing at the position.

Leech studied the plotted position of the stricken ship. His ruddy, leathery and lined face was motionless as he stared at the chart.

"What the devil is he doing out there?" the captain asked stolidly.

"He says he was attempting to make a passage to Hai-k'ou from Manila during the storm when heavy seas caved in one of his hatches and they began taking on water," Heyerdahl explained.

"Lovely," Leech said, coldness in his tone. "He's only ninety miles north-northwest of the typhoon's center." He wondered whether or not he should risk his own crew and vessel in the face of a killer typhoon to go in for a rescue.

But this was not his only concern.

Just then a sleepy Briscoe arrived.

"Good morning, Captain. Mornin' Mike."

"Good morning, Jimmy," Heyerdahl replied.

"What's the trouble?" Briscoe asked.

"We just received a Mayday," Heyerdahl explained. "A Panamanian ship is sinking right about here." He pointed to the position on the chart.

Briscoe stepped toward the table and looked at the chart.

Captain Leech asked, "Mr. Bris-coe, what is your opinion of this situation?"

Briscoe studied the chart and realized what the Old Man was worried about.

"Oh, boy. They're only twenty-five miles northeast of Macclesfield Bank. A 'great' place to be in a typhoon," he said sarcastically. "If she doesn't sink first, the typhoon's northeasterly winds will push her right over the bank before we could reach her. It's bad enough they're near the typhoon's center, but to attempt a rescue in the middle of a poorly charted area like that..." Briscoe shook his head.

Both men stared at the chart. Macclesfield Bank was a submerged atoll about 75 miles long and 35 miles wide. It was dotted with shoals. For most small, shallow draft vessels traveling through the region the shoals posed no problem. However, for a ship the size of the *Majestic Prince's,* with her deep, thirty-six-foot draft, they posed a serious threat.

"I agree, Mr. Bris-coe. What do you think we should do?" Leech asked, looking to see if his own opinion concurred with that of his venerable chief officer's.

Briscoe sighed. He looked at the chart and then at Leech. He said, "It's a life or death situation, Captain. If no one else responds to their distress, then we're the only ones in the area who can help. We must go. Our GPS will help us avoid the charted shoals. It's the uncharted ones that we have to worry about."

Leech thought for a moment and nodded. The GPS, or Global Positioning System, would provide them with constant satellite position fixes. They would know exactly where they were in relation to the charted shoals at all times. Any set and drift would be immediately detected.

He then ordered, "Mr. Heyerdahl, call the engine room and tell them we're going to speed up."

"Yes, sir," Heyerdahl replied and picked up the telephone.

Leech said, "If we can average ten knots in this mess, we'll be there some time after eight in the morning."

Briscoe nodded. He then walked to one of the forward bridge windows and looked out into the miserable dark. "Daylight rescue. Good timing," he said.

Just then more spray from the bow was hurled aft by the wind and slammed into the bridge windows.

■ ■ ■

They informed the captain of the *Stellar Polaris* they were on their way. Based on the wind and swell conditions, they gave an ETA of 0800 the next morning. If they could average ten knots, it would take them a little over eleven hours to reach the *Polaris.* If they could average better, they'd be there sooner.

The swells from Typhoon Angela were twelve-feet tall when the *Majestic Prince* began her rescue mission. The huge ship rode poorly, constantly pitching up and down, her bow pounding the seas as she fought the swells. Angela's fifty-knot winds were not a problem. They were from the east and on the ship's port quarter; as they neared the storm they would shift to the northeast, and the ship's stern. During the first several hours of the trip the *Prince* managed to average twelve knots, but as the night went on and the swells increased in size, the pounding reached alarming intensities. The bow was slamming the seas hard, sending severe, heart-stopping vibrations throughout the entire ship. The ship had to be slowed or else structural damage would occur.

The speed reduction stretched their original ETA by only an hour and Leech and Briscoe hoped they could get there in time before the *Polaris* went down. They were dismayed, however, when communication with the ship was lost shortly after sunrise. They feared she was gone.

Later that morning they arrived ten miles northeast of Macclesfield Bank and found no traces. Swells had increased to twenty-five feet. They assumed the *Stellar Polaris,* if she hadn't yet sunk, or her lifeboats had been blown to the southwest towards Macclesfield Bank. They continued onward.

On the bridge were Leech, Heyerdahl, third mates Short and Lindvall, and AB Silalahi. The entire bridge shuddered from hitting one swell after another. Heavy spray flew aft from the bow and slapped the windows. Leech and Lindvall searched the horizon with binoculars. Silalahi was at the helm. Heyerdahl manned the radar. Short watched the depth recorder.

The radar screen was filled with glowing, green globs. These were echoes from the swells and waves. Despite this sea clutter, Heyerdahl noticed something on the screen. It was a small, yet defined, intermittent pip, off to starboard.

"I have something on radar, Captain," he said.

"Where is it?" Leech asked.

"Bearing 210 at 12 miles."

Leech looked through his binoculars. "I don't see anything yet."

As they approached the large atoll, Heyerdahl noticed the target was now appearing with every sweep on radar amidst the sea clutter.

"It's too small to be a freighter, Captain," Heyerdahl observed. "It couldn't be a lifeboat, either. The sea's too rough for the radar to detect something that small. It must be a small ship."

"Or a sinking one," Leech said. "Dead slow ahead."

"Dead slow ahead," Lindvall repeated as he hurried to the engine throttle control and pulled the stick back to slow the vessel.

"Let's see what it is."

■ ■ ■

It was blustery on deck. Briscoe was busy making preparations. With him were Knuckles, Hillert, Hawkins, and Moxey.

The bosun said to Briscoe, "I sent Dell and Bickle forward to get the cargo nets you wanted. They'll be back in a few minutes."

"Good. Have the nets secured aft of both gangways and then drop them over the sides; all the way down to the water's edge. We'll need line." To Hillert he said, "Go forward and bring back a coil of one-inch line and a couple of heaving lines.

"On my way," the seaman said and left.

"Bosun, have the two sailors collect all of the ship's spare life rings. Bring them back here where we can get to them in a hurry."

As he spoke to Knuckles, Briscoe glanced at Moxey. She was looking attentively at him.

Briscoe concluded with, "Be sure to lash them so they don't blow away."

"Right," Knuckles said, and he turned to the two sailors. "Hawkins, Moxey...you heard the man. Spare life rings. They're in the forward cage."

The wind was now blowing out of the northeast at sixty-five knots. The slowness of the ship made her highly susceptible to the wind and she yawed sluggishly. The *Majestic Prince's* forty feet of freeboard acted like a giant, nine hundred and thirty-six-foot sail.

Helmsman Silalahi had to use large amounts of rudder to keep the ship on course.

Suddenly, a black line began to appear on the depth recorder. "We're on the graph paper, Captain," Short announced. "1300 fathoms."

"Very well," Leech acknowledged. "Mr. Heyerdahl, let's keep a sharp lookout. He's out there somewhere."

"Yes, sir," Heyerdahl said as he moved from the radar to the window and picked up a pair of binoculars. He scanned the horizon in the direction of the radar target, looking closely into the troughs of the swells.

"The bottom is rising quickly now, Captain," Short reported. "Five-hundred fathoms."

"Thank you," Leech responded.

A half hour later the depth line had risen all the way up to thirty fathoms.

"Thirty fathoms, Captain," Short reported. He looked from the depth recorder to Captain Leech and said, "Captain...we're here. Macclesfield Bank."

"Very well. Plot our position every five minutes, Mr. Short."

"Yes, sir."

With Short monitoring the depth recorder to detect any further rapid rises in the sea's bottom and using the GPS system to plot the ship's position, Leech guided his huge ship over the atoll and through the charted shallow areas.

Heyerdahl swept the horizon with his binoculars and then stopped. "Got it!" he called out.

"Where?" Leech asked.

"Point-and-a-half to starboard," the second mate reported. Heyerdahl walked to the radar and glanced at the screen to check the *Polaris's* distance. "He's five miles. That's our visibility."

Leech looked through his binoculars.

Heyerdahl returned to the window and looked through his binoculars again. He said, "I'll be damned. No wonder it looked so small on the radar."

Leech saw the wreck, too. "It's half-submerged."

The *Stellar Polaris's* bow was below the surface and only the after house, the stern, and less than one hundred feet of main deck remained above water. The freighter was angled alarmingly downward like a submarine commencing a steep dive.

"Captain, I see a couple of lifeboats half-way between us and the ship," Heyerdahl said.

The *Polaris's* two lifeboats floated in the water nearby. Men were frantically waving their arms. One boat's engine was apparently inoperable for the other lifeboat was towing it in the *Prince's* direction.

Leech picked up his portable radio.

"Mr. Bris-coe, we have two lifeboats in sight. Prepare to take the survivors aboard on the starboard side. Repeat, starboard side. I'll make a lee."

On the main deck, Dell and Bickle had returned with the cargo nets and were rigging them on the port side with Knuckles. Briscoe was watching when he heard Leech's voice come over the radio. Listening above the noise of the wind, Briscoe understood.

"Survivors on the starboard side. Yes, sir, Captain," he acknowledged. Turning to the Bosun, he said, "Let's forget the net on this side for now. We've got lifeboats on the starboard side. Let's get the other cargo net rigged over there."

"Right away, Mate."

Leech glanced at the chart to see how much room he had to maneuver. They did not have a specific chart for Macclesfield Bank. The chart they were using was not a large scale one and lacked details. According to the chart on hand, he had plenty of room to maneuver for the time being. The huge amount of set and drift the ship was experiencing due to the high winds and swells made it a constantly changing situation.

"Mr. Short, keep a sharp eye on that depth recorder. There may be a shoal out there that isn't on our chart."

"Yes, sir," the third mate said.

Returning to the wheelhouse, Leech ordered, "Hard left!"

Helmsman Silalahi repeated the order. "Hard left."

The ship began to swing to port.

"Stop engines. Bow thruster hard to port," Leech ordered.

"Stop engines. Bow thruster hard to port," Lindvall repeated the order and moved the engine throttle stick to the stop position while simultaneously shoving the bow thruster controller to the left.

■ ■ ■

Leech swung the *Majestic Prince* to the left, pointing her toward the southeast - directly at Angela's center - thus placing the wind directly on the port beam. There was now a suitable lee on the starboard side for the approaching lifeboats. Using reduced engine RPM and bow thruster control, he maintained the heading.

Briscoe directed Dell and Bickle as they quickly lowered the large cargo net over the starboard side and secured it to deck cleats and railing. Moxey and Hawkins returned with life rings. Bosun Knuckles and Hillert then partially lowered the *Prince's* gangway twenty-five feet until it touched the net. Steward Stancy, steward assistants Juan and Jack, and cargo engineer Brad were watching and standing by to assist. The *Polaris's* lifeboats came alongside.

"Drop a line to their boat and secure it over there," Briscoe said, pointing to a cleat forward of the gangway.

Knuckles grabbed the line and dropped it down to the boat.

In the lead lifeboat, the Panamanians grabbed the other end and successfully secured it to their boat. The Panamanians in the towed lifeboat shortened their towline, thus nearly rafting both boats together. This enabled them to cross over to the lead lifeboat. Their crewmembers were anxious to jump onto the net.

Moxey hurried over to help Knuckles. She and Knuckles pulled the line tight and figure-eighted it around a deck cleat. The line began to tighten as the lifeboats drifted aft until they were beneath the cargo net and came to a stop.

"Perfect!" Knuckles said to Moxey.

Without wasting a moment, the crewmembers in the lead boat climbed onto the cargo net with each cresting wave and then transferred onto the gangway. Others skipped the cargo net altogether and jumped on the gangway when their lifeboat rose on each cresting wave. Those men in the towed boat jumped into the lead boat and then followed their shipmates up the cargo net and gangway.

As they stepped onto the *Prince's* main deck, Briscoe was aware that the Panamanians were excited about something. The first man to set foot on deck saw Briscoe and assumed him to be in charge. He walked right up to him and began talking to him in a highly excited fashion. As more of the men boarded, they did likewise and surrounded him, all talking at once.

Briscoe had no clue what the man was saying. "What? Wait, wait. I don't understand. No comprende."

The Panamanians gesticulated wildly with their arms and pointed to their sinking ship.

Watching from the bridge wing, Captain Leech saw the commotion on deck. "What the devil is going on down there?" he said to himself.

"What the hell are they talking about, Mate?" Bosun Knuckles asked.

"I don't know. Something about their ship."

Roughly twenty men boarded the *Prince* from the lifeboats. When the last man was safely on the gangway, Briscoe decided it was time to set their lifeboats free.

"Cut the line!" he ordered.

Seaman Hillert cut it.

Another Panamanian crewmember stepped forward and shouted, "No!"

Too late. Both lifeboats were set adrift. They drifted aft and beneath the ship's stern counter where they were crushed against the hull by the rising and falling swells. The last man to jump to safety on the gangway walked up to Briscoe. He identified himself as the ship's captain. His English was poor. Apparently, he was the only one of the group who knew any English at all.

"I am ship's captain. I have men still on ship! One is trapped beneath beam."

"What??" Briscoe asked, stunned. He quickly glanced down at the lifeboats, but all that remained was shattered debris in the *Prince's* wake. "A man is trapped beneath a beam?"

"Yes, yes!" the Panamanian captain spoke, gesticulating wildly. "Big boiler explosion. One man trapped in the engine room beneath I-beam. Three men stay on board try to free him."

"What about burning equipment?" Briscoe asked.

"Huh?"

"Burning equipment; welding equipment," Briscoe said with growing impatience. Gesticulating himself, pretending he was sawing an imaginary object, he shouted above the howling wind, "To cut through the beam!"

The Panamanian captain shook his head. "No good. No good welding equipment aboard."

"Terrific." Briscoe looked up at Leech on the bridge wing and spoke into his radio. "Captain, they still have four men on board. One of them is trapped beneath a beam in the engine room. They need a burning rig right away."

Leech listened.

"They need an acetylene and an oxygen tank," Briscoe said. "I recommended we send a rescue party over there immediately."

Leech thought for a moment. This was a very dangerous request. He glanced over at the *Stellar Polaris*, now only two miles away, and noted that its attitude had not changed much, although it was difficult to tell.

Short continued to watch the depth recorder. The graph was horizontal.

"Fifteen fathoms, Captain, and steady," he reported. "More than enough for our six fathom draft." Glancing at the chart, Short added, "And we're two miles from the nearest charted shoal."

"Very well. Let me know the moment the bottom begins to rise."

"Yes, sir."

Leech spoke into his radio. "All right, Mr. Bris-coe. Prepare your starboard lifeboat. Pick your most experienced people and make sure they wear their life jackets. We'll get a hold of the first assistant and have him prepare the burning rig. Send a few people down to the engine room to give him a hand."

Briscoe looked up at Leech and spoke into his radio. "Yes, sir. Will do."

Leech added, "In the meantime, I'll circle the *Polaris* a couple of times and try to knock down the seas."

"Very good, Captain," Briscoe replied and turned to the two seaman standing beside him. "Bickle and Hawkins, go to the engine room and give the first assistant a hand with a burning rig."

Both men hurried off.

Briscoe continued, "Bosun, take the others and lower the starboard lifeboat to the embarkation deck. I want Dell, Hawkins, and Hillert to go in the boat with me. Make sure they have their life jackets."

"Yes, sir," Knuckles replied and left with the group.

To Steward Stancy, Briscoe motioned to the Panamanians and said, "Stew, take care of these people. Get them inside, cleaned up, and fed."

"Right away," the steward said, and he and his assistants led the Panamanian crewmembers aft to the protection of the house.

Turning to the Panamanian captain, Briscoe said, "Captain, will you go back to your ship with us?"

Surprisingly, the Panamanian captain adamantly declined. "Me? Not me. No, no. Ortiz will go. He chief mate."

Briscoe was annoyed with the man's attitude. He seemed arrogant; perhaps he was just plain cowardly. Briscoe asked. "Ortiz? Who's Ortiz? Where's Ortiz?"

The captain looked around the deck until he spotted his chief mate. "Ortiz!" he called out. "Ortiz!"

A scrawny, little man in his late thirties, stepped forward.

Briscoe said, "You go back to ship with us."

The Captain translated. Ortiz nodded that he would.

■ ■ ■

Fighting wind, swells, and the threat of an uncharted shoal, Captain Leech circled the *Stellar Polaris* several times in an attempt to knock down the twenty-five-foot seas. Maintaining a distance of a quarter mile from the sinking ship, he was reasonably successful and the seas within his circle had temporarily subsided to about fifteen feet.

Third mate Short continued to monitor the depth recorder graph for any sudden changes in the bottom. Once over the atoll, the depth had remained at fifteen fathoms, which was plenty for the *Prince's* six fathom depth.

A short time later the *Majestic Prince's* starboard lifeboat was lowered to the embarkation deck and the men worked fast loading it. Two, long, heavy cylinders of oxygen and acetylene were brought out on deck and carried into the boat, along with hoisting straps, two hundred feet of welding hose, a cutting torch, a block and tackle arrangement in which to hoist the cylinders aboard the sinking ship, and several flashlights for the rescuers to find their way around in the dark since the *Stellar Polaris's* generator was dead.

Briscoe, speaking into his radio, said, "Captain, we're ready down here."

"Very well. Stand-by then," Leech responded. "I'm trying to maneuver the ship in as close as I can to make a good lee for you. It'll be a few more minutes."

"Very well, sir. Standing by."

"Mr. Short, how are we looking?" Leech asked his third mate.

Third mate Short plotted a position from the GPS, and then glanced at the depth recorder.

Short said, "We're still in the clear, Captain."

Leech maneuvered his ship in closer to the *Polaris,* thus shortening the distance and time the lifeboat would have to travel.

Six men were going on the perilous journey over to the *Stellar Polaris.* Briscoe, first assistant engineer Dirk Mainline, and seamen Arnie Dell, Darryl Hawkins, and Max Hillert. Ortiz, the *Polaris's* wiry but strong chief mate, was going as well to show them where the injured man was located.

Awaiting word to launch from the bridge, Briscoe and the others gathered on the starboard boat deck. The starboard lifeboat hung over the side, it's gunwale resting hard against the embarkation deck. Briscoe tied the straps on his life jacket and glanced at each member of the group as they arrived. He then noticed that everyone in the boat crew, except Hillert, was wearing their life jackets.

"Hillert, where's you life jacket?" Briscoe snapped with impatience.

Embarrassed, Hillert said, "Sorry, Mate. I haven't been up to my room yet."

"Go get it. Now!"

"Be right back," Hillert said. He took off and ran up the ladder to his room.

Briscoe looked out at the *Polaris*. The two ships were less than a quarter of a mile apart.

Speaking into his radio, Leech said, "Mr. Bris-coe, this is the best lee we can make for you without being blown down onto that shaky bastard. Once you're over there, we'll move the *Prince* around to the downwind side of the *Polaris* so you won't have to fight the swells coming back. I doubt you'd make it, anyway."

Briscoe raised his radio's mike to his mouth and acknowledged, "Very good, Captain."

"Lower your boat when ready," the old man ordered.

Briscoe responded, "Aye, sir." To the others, "All right, everyone. Let's go."

The men began crossing from the main deck into the lifeboat and sat down on the thwarts.

Max Hillert ran to his room, two decks up, and grabbed his life jacket. Rushing back, he hurried down the ladder to the boat deck when all of a sudden the rolling of the ship caused him to slip and fall. He bounced down the steel steps on his rear end and then on the very last step his right foot caught a railing stanchion and swung him around. Briscoe heard the noise and turned to see the able seaman lying there on the main deck.

Dell and the others seated in the lifeboat heard Hillert fall and they all looked in his direction.

"Are you all right?" Briscoe asked, hurrying over to the man.

Knuckles, Steward Stancy, and Moxey, who were assisting with the lowering of the boat, rushed over to help.

Hillert moaned and grimaced in pain as he stood up. "I twisted my ankle, Mate. I don't think I can walk. I'm sorry, Mate."

"Damn!" Briscoe said to Stancy, "Steward, take care of this man."

"Right, Jimmy. Come on, Max," Stancy said as he helped Hillert up off the deck and towards the house.

As they were leaving, Briscoe said, "Max, give me your life jacket. We're going to need it."

The hobbling AB stopped, removed his jacket, and gave it to the mate.

"Shit, now I need another AB." He turned to Moxey and said, "Greta, go to the bridge and relieve Silalahi. Tell him I need him in the boat *now*."

"Let *me* go, Mate," she said.

"What?" Arnie Dell blurted out from the boat.

■ ■ ■

On the bridge wing, Captain Leech wondered what was going on. He was becoming impatient. The lifeboat still hadn't been launched and people down there in the vicinity of the boat seemed to be disorganized.

"What's the hold up down there, Mr. Bris-coe?" he asked. "I can't hold this lee forever."

Briscoe heard the old man's voice crackle over the radio and ignored his question. He looked at Greta and was hesitant. His stern, blue eyes studied the face of the attractive, young woman standing before him. Her rich, rusty red hair which was done up in two ponytails was blowing in the wind as she beseeched him with her eyes. Ever since the day she had come aboard, he had been taken by her. Her presence on the *Majestic Prince* had warmed his heart. He tried to look past how adorable she was standing there in her moment of sincerity. In the short time since she had been aboard Greta Moxey had proven herself a valuable asset to the deck department. Briscoe didn't want to risk any more lives than necessary, especially that of a woman's - *especially* that of Greta Moxey's - but he knew the diminutive Moxey was as strong as some of the older men on board and he didn't have time to round up someone else. A man was drowning. Several others may die.

"Let me go," she repeated.

"All right then. Here...take Hillert's life jacket. Get in the boat and tend the forward tricing pendant."

Moxey took the AB's life jacket, put it on, and stepped into the forward part of the boat.

Glancing at Greta, Briscoe said to himself, "The Old Man's not going to like this."

No sooner had he thought it when he heard Leech's voice crackle over the radio again. This time he didn't hear the message, but, again, he ignored the call.

"I don't believe this," Dell muttered. He stood up and defiantly began climbing out of the boat. "I'm not going if a woman's going."

Briscoe was the last one left on deck to step into the boat. He blocked Dell's way.

"Dell, you *are* going. We don't have time for this. Now, get back in the boat."

Dell hesitated a moment. He said, "Mate, I don't think she - "

"GET IN THE BOAT!"

Dell snorted, looked like he was going to explode, thought the better of it, bit his tongue, and then did what he was told. He turned around, climbed back into the boat, and sat back down.

Briscoe then stepped into the boat and assumed a position at the stern. He grabbed the release line to the after tricing pendant. Both forward and after tricing pendants held the boat snug up against the *Majestic Prince's* main deck so crewmembers could embark.

"Release the tricing pendants!" Briscoe yelled above the drone of the wind.

Moxey and Hawkins released the forward pendant, while Briscoe and Mainline released the after one simultaneously. With the tricing pendants released, the boat was now free to be lowered.

An angry Captain Leech continued to watch from the bridge wing. When he saw Moxey get into the boat he tried to speak out, but thought his radio battery must be dead since Briscoe didn't seem to hear him. He quickly rushed into the wheelhouse to get another radio.

Briscoe looked at Knuckles who was standing by the winch brake and yelled, "Lower away, Bosun!"

Knuckles nodded, lifted the brake handle on the lifeboat winch, and the boat began its descent.

Briscoe saw Mainline pumping up the lifeboat engine's troublesome, hydraulic starting mechanism. He then heard Leech's voice - a very *angry* voice - crackling over his radio speaker again.

"Mr. Bris-coe, what's that young lady doing in the boat? I don't want her to go!"

"Oh, shit," Briscoe cursed. "Here we go." He couldn't very well ignore the Old Man this time.

From the bow of the boat even Moxey heard Leech over the radio, too. She angrily glared at Briscoe, as if to say "stand up for me."

Dell grumbled aloud, "See? Even the captain doesn't want her in the boat."

Briscoe said to Mainline, "I don't have any time to hoist this boat back up and put her off. There's a man drowning over there." He held his radio to his face and said, "Captain, are you trying to talk to me? You're breaking up."

"I *said* I don't want the woman to go!" Leech repeated harshly.

"Captain, I can't understand a word you're saying!" Briscoe shouted above the howling wind. He looked up at the Old Man who was staring down from the bridge wing. Briscoe waved his radio at him as if to say, "it's no good."

"Damn!" Leech cursed, and then to himself, "You can hear me."

■ ■ ■

First engineer Mainline was still pumping up the engine's hydraulic starting mechanism as the boat was being lowered to the water.

Briscoe asked, "Is that thing going to work?"

The big engineer glanced at Briscoe and didn't say anything. He stopped pumping the starting mechanism, pulled the trip lever, and kicked over the diesel engine. The little engine sputtered for several tense moments and then finally roared to life. He smiled at Briscoe and answered, "Yes."

"Good," Briscoe said with relief.

Turning his attention to the crew, Briscoe said, "Everyone, listen up. It's going to be a rough ride over there. The hardest part, though, will be releasing the boat into this sea. Dell, I want you to stand-by the releasing lever. When I yell 'pull', flip that bar over as fast as you can."

"Right, Mate," the AB said, and then knelt down beside the releasing lever located in the boat's bilges.

"Dirk, you be ready to engage that gear box and hit the throttle so we can get away from the ship *fast*. I don't want to be slammed against the hull."

"I'm ready," the engineer said as he revved the diesel engine once more.

"Greta, Darryl...you two tend that forward block. Make sure it doesn't knock you on the head when we pull the releasing gear." He then looked at Ortiz the Panamanian chief mate. Pointing at the after fall he said, "Ortiz, you and I will tend this block."

The man nodded. He didn't understand English but he knew what needed to be done. The job of launching a lifeboat was basically universal on any ship regardless of language.

Briscoe then looked with uneasiness out at the *Stellar Polaris,* a quarter of a mile away, and the enormous swells that lay in between. They were getting larger as the little boat descended. And this was the *lee* side!

"Oh, boy," Briscoe said to no one, wondering what he was getting them all into.

121

From where he was standing forty feet above, Bosun Knuckles had trouble judging the lifeboat's height above the passing swells. The moment came when the crest of a passing wave grazed the bottom of the boat. He immediately dropped the brake lever, thus stopping the boat's descent. It was best to lower the boat into the trough and it was his intention to do so. The boat, however, had been lowered too much. In the time it took to lower the brake lever, the boat had continued its descent. It was grabbed by the crest of the passing wave and lifted. The boat pitched and rocked violently and the falls went dangerously slack for a second, dropping the heavy metal blocks into the boat.

"Watch that block, Greta!" Briscoe shouted as it looked like Moxey was about to be struck by it.

"I'm okay," she called out, jumping away from it.

The crest then passed and the sea dropped out from beneath the boat, dropping the boat instantly as well, but the falls caught the boat. The cables tightened and the blocks snapped rigidly upward. The six passengers were rocked and jolted. Knuckles immediately lifted the brake lever and began lowering again. As the boat descended she went further into the trough and then another passing crest lifted her up high again. The blocks at both ends of the boat went slack again and slammed downward onto the thwarts at both ends of the boat.

"Dell, pull the lever now!" Briscoe shouted. "Dirk, engage your gearbox. Full ahead!"

With one quick move, the AB pulled the releasing lever and the blocks let go and went flying high above them as the boat dropped into the deep trough that followed. Almost simultaneously, Mainline shoved the gear lever forward and then yanked the engine throttle control out as far as it would go. The engine roared. With the tiller hard over to port and the propeller immersed, the little boat veered off to starboard. Just then another wave was upon them and the boat was upward bound again.

"Watch out for the falls!" Briscoe shouted.

The boat was clear of the after fall, but her stern was swinging rapidly beneath the forward one. It smashed the top of the fiberglass engine cover to pieces and then slammed into the thwart between Mainline and Briscoe, missing them by inches. The following trough dropped the boat again and she continued to move forward, clearing herself of the after fall.

"Greta, get rid of the sea painter!"

Moxey pulled the wooden fid that held the long rope to the boat. The painter jumped over the side. Their last connection to the *Majestic Prince* was gone. They were now moving away from their ship and making way for the *Stellar Polaris.*

"Everybody hang on!"

The ride was incredibly rough. The little boat rode up and down the mountainous swells. For the passengers it was like a ride on a roller coaster. Briscoe worked hard with the tiller to keep the boat on course and to keep it from being flipped over. Fortunately, they were running with the wind and swells.

Everyone else in the boat hung on to either thwarts or the gunwale. The acetylene and oxygen bottles were secured, but they clanged together nonetheless.

Mainline looked up at Briscoe as they rode the enormous waves and shouted above the howling wind, "Jesus, this is some fucking ride, Jimmy! This is better than reality TV!" He then asked, "Just how the hell are we going to hook back up to our falls when we return?"

Briscoe shook his head. "We won't. We'll have to board the *Prince* the same way the Panamanians did and either tow or scuttle our lifeboat."

"Swell," the engineer groaned, his dreadlocks lashing his face. "I don't know about you, Jimmy, but I'm putting down overtime for this day. I don't care what Chief Jacobi says."

"You and me both," Briscoe agreed.

■ ■ ■

Third mate Short continued to watch the depth recorder. The line on the graph remained steady. Leech continued to watch the progress of the lifeboat through his binoculars. Though he didn't look it, he was on pins and needles for he knew how dangerous this rescue was. If the lifeboat capsized or became disabled he had few resources or personnel left on hand to help Briscoe and the others. Part of him wished he hadn't approved the rescue.

Leech put his engines half-ahead and began circling the *Polaris*, again in an effort to knock down the seas for his boat crew.

Despite Leech's efforts, the lifeboat's roller coaster ride over to the *Stellar Polaris* was rough. It was the worst ride any of them had ever

123

experienced in their lives. The little boat was lifted up one mountainous crest and then quickly slid down into the steep trough that followed. The trip over took about fifteen, long minutes.

Approaching the *Stellar Polaris* from its port side, Briscoe went around to the lee side; the starboard side. He maneuvered the boat aft of the *Polaris's* abandoned lifeboat falls where a chain link embarkation ladder with wooden treads was dangling over the side. It swung wildly in the wind. The last man to leave the *Polaris* had been the crewman lowering the lifeboat and he had used the ladder to climb down to it.

"Greta, Darryl, tie up to that ladder when the boat drops."

She nodded, and she and Hawkins waited for the swell's crest to pass. When it did, they quickly threw a line around the ladder, snagged it, and tied it off. The two seamen then cleared out of the way as the ladder came crashing down into the boat as the craft quickly rose on a crest.

"Let's leave the motor running," Mainline said to Briscoe.

"Right," Briscoe agreed.

As the boat was lifted and dropped by the passing swells, Briscoe, Mainline, Hawkins, and Ortiz climbed up the ladder, one by one. Hanging onto this ladder was like riding a mechanical bull, complete with sudden jerks and pulls that threatened to throw them off, but they were prepared and held on tightly. Dell and Moxey remained to tend the boat and to secure the equipment to the hoisting ropes the others would drop down to them.

Briscoe carried a heaving line slung over his shoulder as he climbed. Once on deck, Briscoe handed Ortiz a flashlight. Gesticulating and shouting above the wind, he pointed to the engine room. "Here, take this. You go check on your shipmate. You *check* on your shipmate," he repeated.

Ortiz understood. "Yes, yes," he shouted back. He took the flashlight and headed down to the engine room. The *Stellar Polaris's* emergency generator had long since quit and it would be pitch black inside. In the meantime, until Ortiz returned with a verdict, Briscoe went on the assumption the man was still alive.

"Until Ortiz returns with a verdict, let's get started."

Mainline agreed.

Briscoe dropped one end of the heaving line down to the boat. Moxey and Dell secured it to the block and tackle rig they had brought along.

Briscoe and Hawkins hoisted it and quickly secured it to a stanchion on the next deck up. They then lowered the moving block back down to Moxey and Dell. She secured it to the two canvas straps that were already in place around the acetylene cylinder and then signaled it was ready for hoisting. She quickly backed away from the bottle so she wouldn't be beneath it when the boat was lifted by a swell.

As they were beginning to hoist the cylinder, Ortiz returned. He gave a thumbs-up signal and shouted to Briscoe, "Okay, okay!"

"Great," Briscoe said. Pointing to the line they were now pulling, he said, "Give us a hand here."

Ortiz jumped on the line and he, Briscoe, Mainline, and Hawkins, began heaving up the three hundred pound cylinder. The freeboard on the freighter was only fifteen feet high and they had the first bottle aboard within minutes. The four men stood it up, lashed it to the railing, and then sent the moving block back down to Moxey and Dell where they secured it to the straps that were wrapped around the oxygen cylinder. They then began hoisting it up.

Half way up, the ship rolled and the cylinder slammed hard into the side of the hull.

"Jesus!" Mainline cursed, worrying about a rupture, but nothing happened.

Once the tank was on deck, the men secured it to the railing beside the other tank.

"I'm going up, Arnie!" Moxey said to Dell.

"Why? You're supposed to stay here and help me tend the boat," Dell said.

"They don't need both of us here. You stay and tend the boat," Moxey said. "You can handle it better than I can." Moxey then waited for the next crest and then up the ladder she went.

Dell grumbled but remained. He watched as Moxey climbed the ladder and joined the others. He then positioned himself aft beside the engine control and rudder tiller.

Briscoe saw her coming. He helped her aboard and said, "You shouldn't be up here. I wanted you in the boat."

"You're going to need all the help you can get, Mate. Arnie can handle the boat."

"All right," Briscoe reluctantly agreed. Since she was aboard, there was no point in sending her back down. He then said to the first engineer, "Dirk, we're going to head down and check out the situation. When you get your hoses hooked up, come on down."

"Okay. I'll be right there," Mainline said.

Briscoe then raised his radio. "*Majestic Prince, Majestic Prince.* This is Briscoe. Over."

Leech responded. "Go ahead, Mr. Bris-coe."

"Status update. We've got both cylinders on deck and we're heading down to the engine room now."

"Very well. I'm glad to hear your radio is working again," Leech said with sarcasm. He then added, "Be careful, and good luck."

"Thanks, Captain. Briscoe out."

With flashlights slung around their necks Briscoe, Moxey, and Hawkins left Mainline and led out the cutting torch's two hundred feet of hose. They followed Ortiz down into the bowels of the *Stellar Polaris's* darkened engine room.

Mainline removed the safety cap on the acetylene tank and exposed the cylinder's valve. He then tried to remove the oxygen tank's cap, but it wouldn't budge. He discovered it was badly dented. It had taken the full brunt of the impact against the ship's hull on the way up.

"Shit!" he cursed, and looked around the deck for a bar that he could insert into the cap's slotted sides and, hopefully, leverage it off.

■ ■ ■

As Briscoe, Moxey, and Hawkins went deeper into the darkened engine room, dragging the welding hose with them, they all experienced a feeling of dread. The pounding of the swells outside reverberated ominously throughout the dead, lifeless hull. Their feeling of dread was compounded when they heard water sloshing heavily back and forth below. The sound of a slowly sinking vessel.

"I hope this thing doesn't suddenly drop beneath the sea like a stone," Briscoe said.

Moxey gave him an unappreciative look. "Nice thought, Mate."

As they descended further into the lower engine room, they finally saw a light below.

"There they are," Briscoe said.

They also heard a sawing sound. They followed the sound and the light and it led them to the trapped crewman and the three men who had remained aboard to help. The crewman was pinned beneath a half-submerged I-beam. One of his shipmates was trying, in an almost hopeless, last ditch effort, to hacksaw his way through a half-inch thick, six-inch tall, steel I-beam. He had barely put a scratch on it. Blocks and tackle were hanging loosely around them; polypropylene line floated in the water. Apparently they had tried to hoist the I-beam, but were unsuccessful. The other two men seemed to be waiting helplessly around, holding their flashlights, sadly watching their doomed friend.

Briscoe, Moxey, and Hawkins were not a moment too soon for they found the victim with his mouth only an inch above the water, straining to keep his head lifted and bent back as far as his vertebrae would allow.

From what Briscoe could tell, when the boiler had exploded a support beam had fallen and pinned the man's leg and foot against a pipeline. The beam itself was wedged in between the hull and one of the deck plates. If they could cut through it, the man would be freed.

"We need a hose for him to breath," Moxey said.

"Hose. We need a hose," Briscoe repeated. He then gesticulated the thought to Ortiz and the other crewmembers. "Do you understand me? Hose."

The crewmembers looked blankly at him.

Moxey put her fists one on top of the other, placed them to her mouth, and blew air through her fingers.

Ortiz understood. He and one of the men hurried off to search.

"Where the hell's the first?" Briscoe asked impatiently as he looked up into the dark.

Mainline had found a paint scraper, slid it into the slots on the oxygen cylinder's cap, and pushed with all of his strength. The scraper bent nearly ninety degrees before the cap began to turn. Finally, he was able to remove it. He connected his hoses and opened the two valves. He then took out his flashlight and followed the stretched out welding hose down into the engine room.

When Mainline arrived Briscoe said, "I was just about to come up and see if you were all right. I was beginning to think you had fallen overboard."

"One of the caps was damaged. I had a bitch of a time removing it. We're ready, now. What have we got here?" the first asked, looking over the situation.

"His leg and foot are caught beneath this I-beam and a pipe," Briscoe said, pointing to the section of the beam with his flashlight. "If you cut here, I think we can move the rest of the beam with this block and tackle arrangement they've got hanging here."

"That looks like the best way," the engineer agreed.

"Before you start, let's lash the upper half of the beam so it doesn't slide down on him when it's cut," Briscoe said.

The men helped Briscoe secure the upper half of the beam with the line that was there, and then they secured the lower half to the block and tackle so they could lift it off him. Hawkins and the two remaining Panamanian crewmen stood by to pull on the hoisting line.

"Okay. I think we're ready, Jimmy," Mainline said. "Put something over his head to protect him from the sparks and then everyone look out."

Moxey quickly took off her life jacket and laid it over the man's head. Mainline pulled an ignitor from his back pocket. He opened the two valves on the cutting torch and then lit it off. It's sharp, blue light cut through the air.

Amidst an intensely blinding shower of sparks and smoke as the first engineer burned through the beam, the water continued to slowly creep higher. The trapped man was having trouble keeping his head above the water and was becoming nervous. Briscoe was afraid he might panic.

Moxey saw this as well and did what she could to help the man keep his head up.

"Don't worry," she said soothingly. "Everything's going to be fine. We'll have you out in a jiffy."

The trapped crewman didn't understand a word she said, but her voice conveyed a tone of confidence that he accepted. As she continued to speak she caressed his face and stroked his hair. She made him relax so that the muscles in his neck would relax. This allowed him to raise his head just a little bit higher.

Ortiz finally returned just then with a three-foot long piece of rubber tubing he had found somewhere. They inserted the tube into the crewman's mouth and he was able to relax his head and breath normally as his mouth and nose dipped below the water's rising surface.

Mainline was almost finished cutting through the I-beam. As he burned through the steel with his torch and the sparks illuminated the engine space, everyone present could see the ship sinking before their eyes as they watched the water rise and then cover the trapped crewman's forehead. Moxey continued to stroke his head and the man continued to relax and the rubber tube kept him alive.

"Everybody stand clear of the beam," Briscoe warned as the engineer cut through the last few millimeters.

The moment Mainline cut through, the lower portion of the beam fell off to the side by itself and the crewman was now free. Everyone let out a brief cheer.

"Good job, Dirk," Briscoe said with relief.

"I'm glad something about this trip turned out to be easy," the first engineer quipped as he secured the torch's flame.

Briscoe looked warmly at Moxey and said, "Good job, Greta."

Moxey smiled and winked at him. She grabbed her life jacket and put it back on.

Just then the ship shuddered. This was instantly followed by a loud, deep, groaning sound which seemed to emanate from everywhere in the darkness around them. It was the sound of twisting steel and things crashing above in the house. The downward angle of the ship seemed to have increased. In the luminance of their flashlights, Briscoe and the others looked up into the darkness and then at each other. Time was running out for the freighter. They all knew she could go down at any moment.

"Come on," he said. "Let's get out of here."

The group hurried as fast as they could. The injured man could barely walk. Two of the Panamanian sailors grabbed a hold of his arms and hustled him up the seemingly endless ladders. The others pointed their flashlights on the darkened ladders so the men could see their way up.

As he hurried up the ladder, a nervous Mainline dryly quipped, "I knew there'd be trouble if I cut that beam."

Following close behind him, Briscoe replied, "Do you think it would do any good to weld it back together?"

■ ■ ■

Finally, the group emerged on the starboard side of the main deck. Briscoe squinted as he set foot outside and back into the bright daylight. Wanting to know how much further the ship had sunk, he quickly looked forward down the freighter's deck. He saw the ship was listing more to starboard than before and that the water was much closer to the house than when they had first come aboard. It was then he noticed the boat deck area where they were standing was littered with several paint cans rolling around and pieces of old lumber strewn about. No one gave them much thought; just debris from a sinking ship.

A momentary look of terror swept Hawkins's face. "Mate, where's the ship?"

Briscoe's attention shifted from the rising waterline to the horizon. He did not see the *Prince* either. "Must be on the other side, still circling." He grabbed the mike on his radio and spoke. "*Majestic Prince, Majestic Prince*. We're preparing to get out of here. We have all crewmembers. We'll meet you on the downwind side as planned. Over."

"Roger," Leech responded. "We'll be there by the time you arrive. Just go with the wind, Mr. Bris-coe."

A brief clanging sound was heard above the roar of the wind and an empty paint can suddenly hit the deck. An instant later, before anyone had a chance to look up, a large sheet of plywood crashed to the deck. It missed the first engineer by a foot. The wind then snatched it off the deck and blew it over the side. It flew for hundreds of feet before finally dropping into the ocean.

"Where the hell did that come from?" a stunned Mainline shouted above the shrieking wind.

Everyone tilted their heads backward to see from where the debris had come.

"There!" Briscoe hollered and pointed to the after side of the *Polaris's* wheelhouse.

Looking up, they all saw what appeared to be a temporary paint station up on the bridge. Paint cans, lumber for staging, and plywood were being stowed on the after end of the wheelhouse. Obviously, a bridge deck painting project had been underway before the ship had encountered the storm. Little of the gear was tied down. The securing lines had become chafed, useless, and flapped in the wind. With the additional listing of the ship and the constant driving force of the high winds, the contents of the station were spilling off the bridge deck.

"There goes another one!" Hawkins shouted as they watched a four-by-eight sheet of plywood blow completely away, high above their heads, and out to sea.

"Let's go before someone gets hurt!" Briscoe hollered.

They hurried over to the dangling embarkation ladder and looked down at their boat. Arnie Dell was still there, waiting with the engine running. A couple of Panamanian paint cans had jumped into the boat to keep him company.

"Come on! Shit's flying everywhere!" Dell yelled up to them. "Hurry up!"

They quickly lowered the injured man down to the boat using the same block and tackle that had been employed for hoisting the cylinders aboard. Dell moved forward in the lifeboat, took hold of the man's legs, and gently helped him into the rising and falling boat. The rest of the group then quickly boarded and they cast off their line, leaving the *Stellar Polaris* to her fate.

As they pulled away, more cans and lumber fell into the water around them. Everyone protected their heads with their hands and arms, and by laying low in the boat.

"The *Prince*!" Greta shouted.

They all looked up and there was their ship in the distance, approaching from the left.

"Man, I can't wait to get back onboard her," Mainline said.

They were several hundred feet away from the *Polaris* when Dell raised his head to see the *Prince*.

"Home, sweet home," he said upon seeing the huge, LNG carrier. As he spoke the *Majestic Prince* suddenly changed direction. "Hey, Mate, he's changing course."

Briscoe and the others all watched, puzzled by the maneuver, as the *Prince* veered sharply to its right. It seemed to be heading directly for the *Stellar Polaris*.

As he watched the ship swing, Dell stood up and asked, "What's he doing, Mate?" He then turned to Briscoe for an answer when something out of the corner of his eye caught his attention.

"Look out!" Dell shouted.

It all happened in an unbelievable flash.

Dell had just turned to face Briscoe. Without turning around to find out why, the sudden look of terror in Dell's face caused both Briscoe and Mainline to instinctively drop to the deck just as a large sheet of plywood grazed their heads. It skipped along the boat's gunwale for a few feet and then body-slammed Dell head-on. The typhoon force winds continued to drive the plywood and Arnie Dell was hurled effortlessly over the side.

On Briscoe's radio Leech's voice crackled, "Lifeboat one, *Majestic Prince*. Come in."

■ ■ ■

The *Majestic Prince* was having a problem. During the course of the rescue mission, as the *Prince* circled the *Stellar Polaris*, both vessel's were setting rapidly to the southwest by Typhoon Angela's northeasterly winds. Captain Leech thought his ship would be safely clear of shoals for the duration of the rescue, but third mate Short announced the black line on the depth recorder was suddenly rising.

Leech walked over to the chart table as Short put down a current GPS position. Both men looked at the depth recorder. The black depth line was still rising, and quickly.

"There shouldn't be a shoal here according to the chart, Captain," Short noted.

"But there is," Leech said as he patiently watched the depth recorder. "*This* shoal is not on *this* chart. The charted depth doesn't match what the depth really is."

"What do you want to do, Captain?" Heyerdahl asked.

"We have no choice," he said calmly. "We have to stay away from it. Let's alter course to starboard. Hopefully, that'll give us some distance from it. Head directly for the *Polaris*, Mr. Heyerdahl."

"Aye, sir."

"I'll get a hold of Mr. Bris-coe and tell him not to go any further."

Leech's voice crackled over Briscoe's radio. "Lifeboat one, *Majestic Prince*. Come in. Over."

Briscoe didn't have time to answer. Blood was dripping down from the top of his head while he and everyone else onboard the lifeboat searched the surface for Arnie Dell.

"He's gone!" Hawkins shouted. "Dell's gone!"

Dell had disappeared in a trough behind the lifeboat. A moment later he reappeared.

"He's there!" Moxey shouted, pointing at Dell.

"I see him!" Briscoe hollered back to her.

Dell's body was limp in the water thirty feet away. The collision with the plywood had either knocked him unconscious or he was dead. If he was alive, he could at least breathe. His life jacket had done its job, fortunately, and had turned his body face up, just as it was designed to do.

"Everybody hang on. I'm turning around."

"Won't we flip over if we do that?" Mainline asked, worry in his voice.

"Not if I do it right," he replied. Briscoe waited for the moment when the next crest passed. When it did, he shoved the tiller hard over. "Here we go!"

The little boat slid into the trough and turned around just as the next swell rolled in. Briscoe eased off the tiller and headed directly toward Dell.

"Good job, Jimmy. That was scary. Can you do it again?" Mainline asked, glancing behind him at the *Majestic Prince*.

"You better hope so," he replied. To his crew, "Greta, get a line ready to throw to him. Darryl, Ortiz, get ready to grab him as we pass."

"Lifeboat one, *Majestic Prince*. What's happening over there?" Leech asked. He had seen the lifeboat do a one-eighty.

Briscoe finally responded. "We lost Dell over the side, Captain. We're heading back to get him."

"Understood," Leech said. "When you get him back, stay in that area. We've got a shoal we're trying to avoid. We'll come to you."

"Okay, Captain. Will do. Briscoe out."

Captain Leech had been correct earlier when he said he didn't think the little boat could make it running against the seas. The boat fought hard, but made only slight headway. The good news was Dell's body was being blown in their general direction. As Dell and the boat approached each other, however, they were on different tracks. Briscoe tried to maneuver the boat closer to him, but it was never close enough for the boat crew to grab hold of him. He was only fifteen feet away.

Briscoe knew what needed to be done. "Dirk, slow the boat down and take the tiller. I'm going to get him."

"What? Wait, I don't know how to steer this thing," the burly engineer said, reducing the throttle. The boat instantly slowed.

"I'll do it, Mate," Moxey said. She picked up one of the lines she and Hawkins had made up earlier.

"All right," Briscoe said. "Come on back here and take the tiller."

"No," she said. "I meant that I'll go and get him."

"Definitely not, Greta!" Briscoe said adamantly.

She handed the end of the line to Hawkins and said, "Tie this off."

"Greta! No!" Briscoe shouted.

Before they could discuss it any further, Moxey had taken the line and jumped in the turbulent water.

"Damn it!" Briscoe cursed.

Between heaving seas, wind spray, and her water-soaked clothing, the relatively short distance of fifteen feet to Dell was a difficult distance for Moxey to swim. It would have been so for anybody. She reached him, though, and quickly tied the end of the line to his life jacket strap.

"Okay! Heave away," she yelled, hanging on to him.

Just then Dell's eyes opened. Her shouting near his ears woke him up.

"What's happening?" Dell said, groggily.

Another sheet of plywood slammed into the water off to their right, only seven feet away. More saltwater was splashed into their eyes.

"Geez," she said, "that was close."

"Plywood," Dell mumbled. "I hate three-quarter inch plywood."

"Hey, he's awake!" she shouted to the others.

While Briscoe manned the tiller and held the boat steady in the seas, the others pulled in the line and brought both Moxey and Dell right up alongside. They then, with great difficulty, pulled his two hundred pound body from the water. His drenched clothing and soaked life jacket made him heavier. Hawkins, Mainline, and two of the Panamanians each grabbed a piece of him and pulled up and over the boat's starboard gunwale while Briscoe, Ortiz, and the other two Panamanians stayed on the port side to keep the boat balanced. Dell, himself, was able to assist a little by pulling himself over the gunwale. Once over the gunwale, he rolled into the boat like a beached walrus.

The group then immediately shifted their attention to Moxey. The four men grabbed and hauled her aboard. Compared to Dell, her light weight made her a snap.

From where he stood on the stern, Briscoe could tell Arnie Dell's nose was broken and that he was in pain. It was bloody and flat. He called out to him, "Dell, is anything broken besides your nose?"

"I don't think so, Mate. My head and ribs feel sore, but that's all."

All hands were now aboard. Briscoe had been watching the *Stellar Polaris* as it drifted down toward them. They were now only a few hundred feet from the sinking ship. He was preparing to turn his lifeboat around after the next crest, when he realized how close the *Majestic Prince* was. It, too, was bearing down on them.

He picked up his radio mike. "Briscoe to Captain. We've recovered Dell. He's banged up a little, but he's alive."

"Very good, Mr. Bris-coe. Stay where you are. We're going to make a lee for you right here."

"That would be fine, Captain," Briscoe replied, "but won't the *Polaris* be too close?"

"We'll have to chance a close encounter with it. I'd rather hit something I can see than something I can't," Leech said, referring to the shoal. "I'm going to come in between you and Polaris. We'll take you on the port side. The bosun's rigging a sea painter for you there now. Get your people aboard as quickly as possible so we can get out of here."

"Roger, Captain. We have two injured. Have the bosun ready with lines to hoist them, too."

Briscoe maintained the lifeboat's heading as it slid up and down the mountainous waves. They all watched as the *Majestic Prince* cut in between them and the *Polaris*. The side of the *Prince* was now only twenty feet away and created an instant lee for them. Still, it was a roller coaster ride, though not as bad.

As he approached the LNG carrier, Briscoe eyed the sea painter hanging from the main deck. Bosun Knuckles had lowered the line to the water's edge just aft of the port gangway. It was secured to a cleat on deck. The cargo net hung over the side just aft of the gangway. Working the tiller, Briscoe maneuvered the little boat toward the sea painter.

"Greta, Darryl. Grab the painter!"

Using the eight-foot long boat hook, the two seamen retrieved the line and tied it to the boat's forward thwart. They then began pulling themselves forward as close as possible to the *Prince's* gangway. The little boat slammed into the hull several times. Finally, they were alongside the cargo net. Bosun Knuckles and other crewmembers were standing by on deck to give a hand.

"Dell, are you up for this?" Briscoe asked the AB. "We can send down a stretcher."

"Yeah, Mate, no problem. I can do this," Dell said, his face grimacing as he endured pain.

"Okay, then. Greta, Dell, Darryl, Ortiz, and you three men...Go!" Briscoe shouted, and waved at them to leave. "Give Dell a hand!"

One by one, the seven climbed onto the rope net and then onto the gangway's platform leaving Briscoe, Mainline, and the injured Panamanian behind.

Briscoe shouted up to Knuckles, "Bosun, drop down a line!"

Knuckles nodded and a moment later a line was dropped into the boat. Briscoe quickly tied a bowline with a large eye and then passed it over the injured Panamanian's head and under his arms. The Panamanian grabbed a hold of the line and when the boat rose on the crest of a passing swell, Briscoe signaled to Knuckles and the others on deck to heave up. The injured man was lifted and within seconds was successfully grabbed by Ortiz and Darryl who were standing on the gangway platform.

As soon as the injured man was safely on the gangway, Briscoe and Mainline left the lifeboat. They both scrambled up the cargo net and then onto the gangway. Setting foot on the main deck, Briscoe looked up at the bridge wing and gave Captain Leech a thumbs-up sign.

Leech returned the thumbs-up sign. With all hands safely aboard, Leech ordered, "Full ahead, hard right!"

"Full ahead, hard right," Heyerdahl repeated.

Most everyone on deck, including Briscoe, ran over to the starboard side to see how close the *Polaris* would come. As the

Majestic Prince sped up, they all watched as the abandoned ship passed about one hundred feet near the stern.

Captain Leech watched with relief from the bridge wing. He returned to the wheelhouse and said, "Mr. Short, as soon as we're clear of this shoal, plot a course for Singapore."

"Yes, sir," Short responded as he continued to monitor the depth recorder.

Later, Leech swung his ship around and headed off Macclesfield Bank, towing the ship's lifeboat alongside by its painter.

Two hours later the depth recorder graph line plummeted off the scale. The ship was safely out of harm's way.

■ ■ ■

Arnie Dell was sent to his bed immediately upon returning from the sinking ship. Crewmembers helped the AB to his room. A short time later, Briscoe arrived with a medical kit and examined him. He found his nose was, indeed, broken and that several of his ribs were tender to light pressure. He suspected Dell either had cracked or broken ribs in addition to his broken nose. The chief mate cleaned up and bandaged Dell's nose, and gave him a painkiller.

"How do you feel?"

"Like I was run over by a truck," Dell replied. He was still in pain; his upper body sore.

"We'll have to put you off in Singapore for treatment. Aside from prescribing bed rest and painkillers, there's not much more I can do for you."

"Singapore, huh? I can live with that inconvenience," Dell joked. He grimaced as he laughed.

"Don't laugh," Briscoe advised.

Greta Moxey knocked on the door.

"How are you doing, Arnie?" she asked, stepping in the room.

"My nose is broken and the mate thinks I have cracked or broken ribs. Other than that, I guess I'm okay."

"Could be worse," she offered.

"Greta...I heard you jumped in to save me. Even after the Mate told you not to. That was brave of you."

137

"Well, I thought he was too busy driving the boat to swim after you himself. Someone had to."

"Thanks. I owe you big time. I'm sorry about my rotten attitude toward you since you've been aboard. You sure proved me wrong."

"Apology accepted."

"I'm sorry about your Spandex, too," Dell confessed.

"So, it was you," she said. "I suspected it."

"Yeah, it was me."

"What happened to your Spandex?" Briscoe asked as he gathered up his medical supplies.

"It disappeared from the laundry room the day after the meeting in your office," Moxey said. "I went down to move my clothes to the dryer and it was gone." Turning to the AB, she asked, "Where is it?"

"Over the side," he answered sheepishly. "I'm sorry. I was upset. I promise I'll replace it, Greta. Honest."

Greta nodded with approval. "I'll hold you to your word. That was my favorite outfit."

"Naughty, naughty, Arnie," Briscoe gently admonished him. He headed for the door with the medical kit in hand. "Get some rest."

"Thanks, Mate."

"No problem."

"Hey, Mate, how's that guy doing who was trapped in the ship?" Dell inquired.

"He's okay. His ankle's broken, but he's resting comfortably. You do the same."

■ ■ ■

The Panamanian captain turned out to be loud and rude; an arrogant, to-hell-with-the-world-I'm-the-Captain type. The only English word he seemed to know well was the "F" word. He immediately wanted to send a telex to his company and then demanded his own quarters. He obviously didn't want to be with his crew whom he considered to be lowlifes and swine.

He had demanded of Steward Stancy a private room with a bath. Stancy looked at the ass in amazement. The only bath on the entire ship was in the ship's hospital.

"What does he think this is? A cruise ship?" Stancy said to Fritz the cook.

Stancy called the captain and told him of the belligerent man's request.

Captain Leech refused both requests as he had his own telexes to send first, and that the man was in no position to demand anything. Leech took an instant dislike to the man's arrogance and, even though he could have easily put the captain up in the vacant owner's room across the passageway from his own room, he had no desire to do so. In his view, any man foolish enough to attempt a passage from Manila to Hai-nan Tao during a typhoon was hardly worthy of being considered a captain.

"Give him a blanket and let him lay with his crew on the deck of the lounge," he said to Stancy.

The *Majestic Prince* proceeded slowly toward Singapore. Typhoon Angela continued to be a vicious storm and tossed and bounced the ship without mercy. The *Prince* was boxed in between Angela to the southwest and Macclesfield Bank to the northeast. The best Leech could do was put the ship on a course skirting down the southeast side of Macclesfield, thus staying as far from the typhoon as possible. The winds and seas picked up tremendously as the ship approached the storm's center and passed within sixty miles of it. At its worst, the seas were running over thirty-five feet high on the beam and the winds gusted to between eighty and ninety knots. The beam swells caused her to roll heavily, thirty to forty degrees at times; each roll snapping the ship back to vertical with frightening force. Leech eased the rolling by heading further to the south and placing the swells on the port bow.

With each roll, the pots and pans hanging from an overhead rack in the galley swung noisily back and forth. Crewmembers tried to sleep, but were tossed back and forth in their bunks. The ship's gym was empty. It was no time to workout. The punching bag swung back and forth. A stack of weights rattled in their racks.

Briscoe went to the CCR and made minor adjustments to the ballast, taking on more water, in an attempt to lessen the *Prince's* stiffness. Later, once they were well clear of Macclesfield Bank, Leech altered the ship's heading to starboard to place the swells on the port quarter. She still rolled with vengeance, although with less severity as the ship slowly distanced herself from the storm. The ship pitched deeply countless times and heavy seas broke over her bow, sending water and spray high into the air. The "crashing in the night" sounds were continuous. No one slept that night.

The next day provided a small amount of relief from the rolling and pitching as the swells slowly continued to move further aft due to the ship's progress to the southwest. Steward Stancy, chief cook Sonnenschmidt, and their two assistants had difficulty serving dinner to the crew. Plates and silverware flew off tables and crashed to the floor. Food splattered on the bulkheads nearby. Plates slid across the tables and landed in people's laps.

The ship rolled and the crashing in the night continued.

Chapter Eleven

More of the Same, Except Different

The next day arrived and a tired Briscoe was sitting at his desk attempting to do some paperwork as he listened to *Voice of America* on the radio. Sleep was evasive the night before, but at daybreak his body clock and his work schedule forced him to get up.

His telephone rang and a weary Briscoe answered it. "Hello."

He noted an equally weary-sounding voice on the other end. It was Captain Leech.

"Mr. Bris-coe, round up the bosun and your gang. We have Vietnamese refugees on the port bow. Prepare to take them aboard."

Briscoe couldn't believe it. This is turning out to be some trip, he thought.

To Leech, he merely said, "Yes, sir, Captain. I'll get everyone out there."

■ ■ ■

"There must be over a hundred refugees crowded onto that thing," Briscoe said to Bosun Knuckles as they watched the tiny nine-meter craft come along the port side. "Prepare to take them aboard."

Most of the people on the little boat were standing since there was no room to sit or lie. All were exposed to the nasty elements for there was no house for protection. Most were women and children. There were several infants as well. A few women were noticeably pregnant. They were all waving and shouting euphorically at the *Majestic Prince.*

Unlike the Panamanian sailors, most of the Vietnamese refugees were weak and unable to jump onto the gangway platform when their boat was lifted by a cresting sea. Instead, Briscoe had his men lower a heaving line with the eye in it down to them. The people were instructed to place it over their heads and under their arms, and then hold tight. When a wave crested and their boat was lifted, one person at a time was hoisted by the sailors on deck up to the ship's gangway where they were grabbed by Darryl Hawkins and cargo engineer Brad Bensinger who were on the platform waiting.

One by one, they climbed the gangway and stepped aboard. One by one, Briscoe noted their poor condition. They were all soaked to the skin, weak, and exhausted. They must have been out there a long time, he thought.

Working on the gangway platform, the muscular Hawkins helped every single one of the refugees aboard. The men on deck would pull the heaving line, lift the person, and Hawkins would reach down, grab their arms, and pull them up the rest of the way to the gangway. For the delicate infants that came aboard, Hawkins laid chest-down on the gangway platform and the refugee men in the boat hand-passed their babies to him one at a time with each crest of a swell. It was work that required precision and perfect timing. One wrong move and a little life would be lost. Hawkins handled the delicate creatures with great care in the midst of the maelstrom that surrounded them, picking them up and passing them on to Bensinger who stood over him on the platform. Bensinger, in turn, carefully passed them on to the next man, who eventually turned them over to Greta Moxey who was waiting at the top of the gangway. Moxey then quickly carried the babies aft to get them out of the menacing elements and into the warmth and safety of the house.

Near the end of the rescue, one emaciated man expired in full view of his family as he reached for the heaving line. He collapsed back into the boat. His wife shrieked, her cries easily heard above the wind. His two children watched, shock and confusion in their eyes. His friends rushed to help him, but it was no use. His body was limp. They checked for a pulse and could find none. They slapped him and shouted at him; they tried mouth-to-mouth; anything to revive him. He was finally declared dead by the others.

Out of a count of one hundred and nineteen people in the boat, one hundred and eighteen refugees made it aboard the safe haven of the *Majestic Prince*. They had had a long, hard journey. Typhoon Angela obviously had not been bargained for in their escape plans.

When the last person set foot on deck, the boat was released with the sole victim remaining. The deceased man's wife and children watched with tired, tearful eyes as the little boat drifted away. It slid aft down the side of the *Majestic Prince* and was destroyed when a passing swell lifted the small craft and crushed it to pieces beneath the ship's massive steel counter.

Refugees were everywhere in the house. Chaos was kept to a minimum as Briscoe and Heyerdahl divided them into groups and located them in the two lounges, the 02 deck recreation room, and the passageways. Steward Stancy instructed his assistants to pass out blankets. Most of the rescued had to share them with three or four others since there weren't enough to go around. The *Prince's* crewmembers donated their own blankets to relieve the shortage. Once the people were grouped, the next order of business was to run them through the showers one at a time to wash off the salt and dirt and any body lice. Towels were passed. At the same time, a massive clothes washing effort was mounted. Some of Briscoe's deck gang went around collecting the refugee's clothing and took it down to the laundry room, leaving roomfuls of naked people waiting for their garments.

Later in the day, a harried third mate Short rushed into the 02 deck passageway and was taken aback by the chaotic scene. It was bulkhead to bulkhead people. Refugees were everywhere! Amidst the crowd he saw Steward Stancy passing out blankets and directing people to find a spot on the deck to call their own.

Working his way over to Stancy, Short asked, "Steward, have you seen the chief mate?"

A frustrated Stancy looked up from what he was doing and answered, "No, I haven't. He's not on this deck. Try the 03 deck or the crew's lounge."

"Thanks. How's it going here?"

"Lousy! There's no room as you can see for yourself."

"Do the best you can, Stew," Short said with encouragement as he patted the steward's arm. He then continued on his search for Briscoe.

"We need a bigger ship!" Stancy called out after him.

Briscoe was on the 03 deck treating a cut on a young boy's arm when Short found him.

"Mate, one of the pregnant women is going into labor."

"Oh, shit," Briscoe cursed. To second mate Heyerdahl, he said, "Mike, you take over here. Keep running them through the showers and get them set up with drinking water. Show them where the heads are, too."

"Will do," Heyerdahl said.

Turning to Short, Briscoe said, "Take the pregnant woman to the hospital and put her in bed."

"Right," Short acknowledged and turned to leave.

"And find Moxey. Tell her to get lots of towels and send her to the hospital, too. I'm going to need all the help I can get."

Briscoe then headed in the opposite direction away from the ship's hospital.

"Where will you be?" Short asked.

"In my office," Briscoe answered, and then hurried away.

■ ■ ■

Briscoe was talking to himself as he entered his office. He went straight for the bookcase on the bulkhead above his desk.

"I haven't been part of a baby delivery in the three years since Katey was born," he muttered nervously. "And even then all I did was run around and snap pictures."

He grabbed the *Medical Aid at Sea* book off the shelf and then ran down to the hospital. When he arrived, Moxey was already there setting up a clean area for the baby. The pregnant woman was in bed and the apprehensive father was standing off to the side watching, not knowing what to do.

"Clarence is sending up more towels," Moxey said.

"Good." Looking at the patient, he asked, "How is she?"

"She's okay, but the contractions are only a few minutes apart."

"Great," Briscoe groaned. "She's almost at the end of her first stage of labor."

Steward Stancy entered the room just then with an arm-full of towels.

Briscoe said, "Set them right there beside the bed, Clarence."

"Okay, Jimmy," Stancy said.

"Thanks."

144

The steward set the towels down and left.

"What do you want me to do?" Moxey asked.

"Try to show her how to breath during contractions to help her ease the pain."

Moxey nodded.

Briscoe then stepped into the adjacent room and sat down on a stool, book in hand. He quickly glanced over the article on birthing in the *Medical Aid* book.

Moxey tried to make the woman comfortable by patting her face with moist washcloths. The woman's contractions were coming with greater frequency. Moxey tried to convey to her the idea of breathing during the contractions. She had reasonable success for the woman finally tried it and found it helped her comfort.

"Mate," Moxey suddenly called out. "She just lost her water. The baby's coming."

Can't she wait a minute until I finish reading the chapter, for chrissakes? Briscoe thought to himself.

He tossed the book on the desk. There was no time for it now. He quickly scrubbed up in the sink and took out a pair of rubber gloves from the supply drawer. He then stepped back into the hospital.

Entering, he saw the apprehensive father watch helplessly.

Putting on the pair of rubber gloves he said, "The main thing to remember about delivering a baby, Greta, is to let nature do the work. We're just here to assist and comfort the mother."

That's the way it had been when Heather gave birth to Gilly and Katey.

Katey.

Little Katey.

The woman screamed just then.

"Oh, God, here we go," Briscoe said.

Minutes passed as they comforted the mother. When the baby's head first appeared, Briscoe immediately thought about the birth of his daughter. He looked at the Vietnamese woman's agonized face and was suddenly reminded of Heather's. Her face was strained with pain. He looked down at the emerging baby and suddenly relived the birth of his daughter.

There was a slap on the feet.

Katey.

There was a cry.

Katey.

Heather's face was smiling.

Heather's happy face, proud and full of joy, then became that of Greta Moxey. He found himself staring at his young AB.

She stood across from him, caressing the woman's face as she pushed. Their eyes met and she smiled quizzically at him, wondering what was going on in his mind.

"Mate?" she asked.

Snapping out of it, he said, "Nothing. Sorry."

The woman pushed and the baby came. Briscoe gently supported the baby's head, neck, and body as it appeared. Greta continued to stroke the woman's head and coached her breathing.

Finally, the baby was clear. Briscoe quickly tied the umbilical cord in two places and snipped it in the middle. He then looked at the baby and was filled with sudden fear. The baby wasn't making a sound.

"Mate, what's wrong with it?" Moxey asked, worried.

"The baby's not breathing," he realized.

Briscoe picked the baby up by the ankles and slapped its feet. Still no sound. He then laid and supported it on his arm, and began artificial respiration. He was sweating.

Moxey coaxed, "Come on, little baby, come on!"

Both the father and mother had a horrible look of fear on their faces.

"Come on! You can do it," Moxey continued to coax.

Just then the baby coughed and began to cry.

"Whew! Oh, boy," Briscoe breathed a sigh of relief.

The parents' look of fear instantly became one of joy.

Briscoe said happily, "Oh...by the way. It's a girl!"

Both parents smiled. Greta smiled, too.

■ ■ ■

Later, when she was resting peacefully with her new baby in her arms, the Vietnamese woman spoke to them. Her husband stood beside her.

"What is you name?" she asked them in barely understandable English.

146

"Mine?" Briscoe asked, puzzled.

"Yes, yes! What is you name?" she asked again, waving her finger back and forth, pointing at both of them.

He looked at Moxey, and then the woman. "Briscoe. James Briscoe," he answered.

The woman then looked at Greta. Greta smiled and said, "Greta Moxey."

"Mox-ie?" the woman asked, her voice rising and hitting the high note of a soprano on the "-ie" syllable. She gave her husband an odd expression.

The slightly built father shrugged and answered, "Moxey."

She then asked, "What is name of ship?"

"Majestic Prince," Moxey answered.

The woman then looked questioningly at Briscoe. Briscoe merely nodded in agreement.

There was a flurry of foreign dialogue between the proud, new parents. Briscoe and Greta heard their names bantered back and forth several times. The ship's name was tossed in there many times as well. The two argued vehemently back and forth and Briscoe was astounded with the mother's high level of energy after having just given birth. It did his "doctor" self-esteem good to know his female patient was doing so well so fast, even though he knew it had been mostly nature's doing.

"What are they talking about, Mate?" Moxey asked.

"I don't know. Maybe it's a Friday night fight."

Finally, after much discussion, a decision seemed to have been reached.

The father looked at both seamen and announced, "We name daughter after you. We call her Kinh Moxey-Briscoe Dien."

"Oh, how sweet," Greta said, beaming. She went over to both parents and hugged them. "Thank you."

Briscoe smiled, slightly embarrassed, and said, "Thank you."

He then shook hands with the proud and happy father and, like Greta, hugged the mother.

As he hugged Mrs. Dien, Briscoe noticed the captain of the wrecked Panamanian freighter peek in through the open hospital door. He had a scowl on his face and walked away.

Briscoe then said to the little baby, "Welcome to America, Kinh Moxey-Briscoe Dien. You're now a citizen."

147

Later, it was time for Mrs. Dien to rest and to leave the couple and their new baby alone. They were doing just fine. Briscoe left the hospital for his room. On his way he passed the Panamanian captain in the passageway. The man still had a scowl on his weathered face.

"Something wrong, Captain?" he asked.

"I do not like those people. They are scum. They crowd everyone's countries. Make big problem for everyone. They should stay home," he replied. Nodding to the ship's hospital, he added, "Each newborn is worthless scum."

Briscoe glared at the man. After all of the effort that was put forth by Briscoe and his crew to rescue the man's crewmembers from his sinking ship, he expected the man to have a little more compassion and respect for human life. He restrained a fleeting impulse to slam the man with his fist.

"So, you're one of those idiot captains who just pass them by, are you?"

"The idiots are the ones who stop to pick them up," the captain retorted with disdain.

"We stopped to pick *you* up," Briscoe said. "You should feel lucky we did. They do."

The captain became silent and merely shrugged.

Briscoe continued. "Captain, while you're on this vessel I want you to keep your mouth closed and be more respectful to everyone onboard. Or else I may just have you thrown over the side."

"Your crew would not do such a thing," the captain said, dismissing Briscoe's threat as idle.

"Perhaps not," Briscoe agreed. He then stepped close to within only inches from the man's face and said, "But I might."

The captain was flustered and found himself at a loss for words.

Briscoe then smiled and walked away. He added, "With your luck, Captain, you'd get picked up by a boat load of refugees. What would you do then?"

The Panamanian skipper said nothing, nor did he say another bad word about anything the remainder of the trip.

■ ■ ■

The night came and Typhoon Angela's winds continued to scream outside. Inside it was relatively quiet considering the large number of people now residing aboard the *Majestic Prince*. Most of the new passengers were dead asleep after their long, severe ordeal at sea. They were stretched out on blankets that lined the passageway and lounge decks. The *Prince* had given them the miracle of renewed life since most had assumed they were doomed.

Greta stepped lightly in between the sleeping as she walked the 03 deck passageway toward the hospital. She wanted to check on Mrs. Dien and her new child. Along the way she looked with empathy upon the women with little children curled up beside them, and the husbands and wives holding tightly to one another. She found a few men still awake. They sat quietly by themselves leaning up against the bulkhead, lost in their own thoughts, as they enjoyed a smoke; their first one in days. They nodded pleasantly as she passed.

Outside the hospital door she heard talking from within, and she entered.

"Hot cross buns, hot cross buns, one a penny, two a penny, hot cross buns; if your daughters don't like them, give them to your sons. One a penny, two a penny, hot cross buns."

Greta found Briscoe sitting in a chair next to the bed reading nursery rhymes to the baby. The newborn was asleep, cradled in her mother's arms. She lay relaxing. Her husband was asleep on a blanket on the floor in a corner. The mother was watching Briscoe, oblivious to what he was saying. However, between the continuous rolling of the ship and his soothing voice, she apparently was enjoying his presence. She looked at Greta and smiled.

Briscoe looked up for a moment, acknowledged her presence with a nod, and then continued.

"A wise owl lived in an oak; the more he saw the less he spoke; the less he spoke the more he heard. Why can't we all be like that wise old bird?"

Greta noted the title of the book in Briscoe's hand. It read *Bonfire of the Vanities* by Tom Wolfe.

"That doesn't sound like *Bonfire of the Vanities*," she said.

Briscoe looked up and smiled. "No. I'm just reciting from memory what I used to read to my kids. They say it's not what you say that counts. It's the rhythmic sing-song of the voice that helps babies go to sleep."

149

Greta was touched.

"Come on, Mate. You need a break."

"Yeah," Briscoe agreed. For the first time during the long, hectic day, he realized he was exhausted. "Come on up to my office, Greta. I'll buy you a soda."

"That sounds good to me."

Briscoe looked at Mrs. Dien and caressed the baby's head.

They said good-night to Mrs. Dien and to tiny Kinh Moxey-Briscoe Dien, left the hospital, and stepped into the crowded passageway. The winds of Typhoon Angela whistled through the poorly sealed weather doors at both ends of the corridor as they walked passed the sleeping souls. The ship continued to roll with regularity.

One deck above they entered his office. Moxey sat down in the chair adjacent to the settee. Briscoe stepped into his bedroom and returned with two sodas from his refrigerator. He handed her one. He then stretched out on the settee, placed one hand behind his head, and sipped the soda with the other. Outside the wind continued to howl.

"I must tell you, Mate, you were wonderful today."

Briscoe chuckled. "'Wonderful?' I've never been called wonderful by a sailor before. Thank you. So were you. I couldn't have delivered that baby without your help, Greta. We made a pretty good team in there today."

"Your baby delivering is much better than your dancing."

"Thanks," he said, rolling his eyes. "I was lucky today, that's all. I was lucky she didn't require a cesarean or deliver the baby with the umbilical cord wrapped around its neck. I was lucky I was able to revive the child."

"What happens next?" she asked.

"To the refugees?"

She nodded.

"Well, we'll drop them off in Singapore. Customs, immigration will come aboard, count them, check them over for disease, and then take them away to a refugee camp. From there, who knows? Some will be allowed to go to the country of their choice. Others will be stuck in the camp until some country agrees to take them. Except for the Diens. Their new daughter is an American so they shouldn't have any trouble going to the U.S."

"You feel sorry for them, don't you?"

He stared at the wall and nodded. "Don't you?"

"Yes, but you seem genuinely saddened."

"I guess I am. Here these people are with no home. They risked their lives and families on a risky sea voyage. For what? A chance to find a better world."

"They've made it, though," she said. "They survived and now they're on their way to a better place. You should be happy. The worst is over for them."

"I know. It's just that I look at them and feel sort of 'guilty' for having what I have while they have nothing. People like us just don't appreciate what we have. Our homes, our cars, our 'VCRs.' When I see people in that situation I sometimes feel I don't deserve what I have."

Greta looked at him and said philosophically, "Chief Mate...it's just the luck of the draw. That's all. Just like the Diens giving birth on an American ship."

"Yeah," he smiled. He raised his soda can to toast. "To the luck of the draw."

"I'll drink to that," Moxey said.

Both drank from their soda cans. Both were tired and there was a long pause. Greta finally broke the long silence and stood up.

She said, "Well, I guess I'd better get some sleep. It's been a long day. Is there anything else I can do to help before I call it a night?"

Briscoe paused for a moment and then looked longingly into her bright, gray eyes. Surprised by this apparent realization he wanted her, Moxey looked into his eyes and studied them to be sure. Briscoe broke off the eye contact and looked away.

"Ah...no," he said quietly.

"Well...good night then, Mate."

Softly, he said, "Goodnight, Greta."

Moxey left the office, leaving Briscoe alone.

Chapter Twelve

Farewells

The *Majestic Prince* worked her way through the heavy swells heading southwest at a snail's pace, slowly pulling away from Typhoon Angela's grip. When the high pressure cell to the north eventually passed and Angela began moving northward, the weather improved, the swells diminished, and the *Prince's* speed increased.

A few days later the *Prince* arrived at Singapore and dropped anchor under blue and sunny skies. The sea was flat calm. It was a welcome sight to all onboard.

Customs, immigration, and quarantine officials swarmed all over the vessel to check the condition of the passengers before taking them into their country. The vessel was delayed for several hours. Arnie Dell and the injured Panamanian were offloaded immediately to a special boat, taken ashore, and then transferred to the hospital. Finally, all of the passengers walked down the gangway and climbed into waiting boats. The Panamanian crew was bound for Changi Airport and then home to the Philippines. Next, a long line of excited refugees were going down the gangway and boarding a Singapore immigration boat. Briscoe, Moxey, and other crew members stood near the top of the gangway saying good-byes and making sure they disembarked safely. The Vietnamese refugees were bound for a refugee camp on the other side of the island.

The proud parents of Kinh Moxey-Briscoe Dien were nearing them as the line slowly progressed. Just before they walked down the gangway, they stepped out of line and hugged Briscoe and Moxey. Greta quickly pulled out her camera and took a snapshot of the couple with their baby. Briscoe and Greta then hugged and kissed little Kinh Moxey-Briscoe Dien herself. The little baby looked at them with wide, curious eyes. Mr. Dien suddenly had a brainstorm and rushed up to Greta while the baby was still in her arms. He took the camera from her hand, stepped back, and snapped a picture of Briscoe and Greta holding little Kinh. He then handed it back to her.

It was a sad moment for all of them. Even though both Greta and Briscoe had given their addresses to the Diens, they knew they would probably never see them again. Briscoe wondered what would eventually become of little Kinh Moxey-Briscoe Dien in this world. Mrs. Dien had tears in her eyes and both she and her husband waved good-bye as they carefully walked down the gangway to the waiting boat.

With the passengers gone, the *Majestic Prince* heaved up anchor and continued on her voyage to the loading terminal in Sumatra. The heaving of the anchor represented the successful end to the dramatic trip.

A lonely, guilt-ridden Briscoe sat at his desk attempting to do paperwork. Despite the activity of the last several days, the birth of Kinh Moxey-Briscoe Dien reminded him of his lost family. He was distracted by the family photos on his desk.

The refugees were not the only ones who were going home. Three weeks later his relief telex arrived. James Briscoe was going home, too.

■ ■ ■

The Japanese pilot boarded the *Majestic Prince* just outside of Tomagashima Suido and took her northward through congested Osaka Bay. The large vessel was escorted by two tugs, as was the usual procedure dictated by Japanese maritime law for ships carrying liquefied natural gas. Four hours later, after maneuvering through the myriads of fishing boats and ship traffic, the *Prince's* mooring wires were secured to the shoreside hooks and she was safely tied up to the Osaka Gas Terminal dock.

In the CCR Briscoe and Bensinger were monitoring the console, taking readings, and talking to Japanese terminal people when Briscoe's relief Barney Hubbard entered the CCR.

153

"All right, Barney. You made it," Briscoe said happily when he looked up and saw the jovial man.

With a shoulder bag slung over his shoulder, an energetic Hubbard responded cheerfully, "I had to. My bank book threw me out of the house again!"

He set his shoulder bag down on the deck and walked to them.

"How ya doin', Jimmy?" Hubbard asked as he shook Briscoe's hand.

"It's good to see you," Briscoe said.

Briscoe knew his side of their relationship was strained and he worked hard not to show it. It had been because of Barney's wife's medical emergency that had prompted him to take the fill-in assignment which resulted in the loss of his family. From that moment on, every time he saw Barney that thought always plagued him. Briscoe hated himself for having that awful thought. He knew that it was a purely emotional response. He forced himself to bury the thought every time it resurfaced. The deep-seated human response to deal with something beyond our control was to blame someone. Rationally, he knew it was no more Barney's fault than it was his own. After all, Barney had been dealing with his own family emergency. Rationally, the entire event was just bad luck. But, still he knew it would take time before he would be able to look at his friend and not think him indirectly responsible for his horrific loss.

Turning to Bensinger, Hubbard said, "Hello, Brad," and shook his hand as well.

"Hi, Barney."

Hubbard turned to the Japanese interpreter who was standing nearby and greeted him. The interpreter returned the greeting.

"How was the vacation?" Briscoe asked.

"Not long enough. It's never long enough. One of these days I'm going to quit and stay home. It was good, though. We went west this time. We visited the Grand Canyon, Vegas, visited some friends on Lake Tahoe, saw Little Big Horn. All that kind of stuff."

"How's Marilee?"

"Just fantastic! The trip did her a world of good," Hubbard replied.

"That's good. I'm glad," Briscoe said with satisfaction.

"Give her a call when you get home. She'd like to talk to you."

"I will," Briscoe assured him.

154

"Listen, I know you probably want to get out of here. I heard you had a helluva tour, what with rescues and typhoons and all."

"We even delivered a baby," Bensinger added.

"Is that right?" Hubbard asked.

Briscoe nodded. "Yes. It was one busy tour."

"The agent says you have an early flight. So tell me what's happening and go."

"Well, all of the systems are working. You've got a good crew, and Leech is still Leech."

Bensinger shook his head. "The day that man changes will be the day they plant him six feet under."

Hubbard's eyes quickly scanned over the status of the cargo console. "Okay...if you've nothing else to tell me, then I've got her. Go catch your plane!"

"All right. It's all yours. Here are my notes for the last four months." Briscoe handed Hubbard a worn-out manila folder. They had been passing the same folder back and forth between them for years.

"Okay. Thanks."

"That's it then. Good-bye, Barney."

They shook hands.

"Have a great vacation," Hubbard said.

"Thank you. I will. Take care, Brad," Briscoe said. "Thanks for your help."

"You, too, Jimmy," Bensinger said.

The two men shook hands and Briscoe hurried out of the control room. Emerging from the CCR, he stopped to take in a breath of fresh air. He was now a free man for four months and like any animal freed from captivity, he was ecstatic; but then, a feeling of emptiness passed through him. He suddenly felt like a man with no place to go and nothing to do.

■ ■ ■

Back in his room, he showered and dressed. He had packed his suitcase the night before and it sat in his office waiting to leave. He cleaned off the bureau top, picking up his watch and wedding ring. For the first time in four months he put the wedding ring back on his

155

finger. He never wore it while on ship for fear of losing it over the side while working on deck. The inscription reflected in his eye.

"I Am Yours."
Heather.
Greta Moxey.
Heather.
Heather.
Guilt.

A knock just then at his door produced the ship's agent who had arrived to fetch him and whisk him away to Kansai International. His flight was leaving that afternoon and they had to move fast.

"Mr. Briscoe. It is time to go," the agent said. "Must get to airport right away."

Briscoe picked up his suitcase. "Let's go."

He stopped by Captain Leech's office where he signed off the ship's articles. Leech then handed him his passport and flight ticket.

"I have something else for you," Leech said. He picked up an envelope off his desk. "It's a letter of commendation I wrote for your efforts during the *Stellar Polaris* rescue. I'm also sending one to Marad. That took a lot of bravery and courage. I'm not so sure I would have done it if I had been in your shoes."

"Thank you, Captain. That's very nice of you."

"I've also written one for the others who were with you; especially young Miss Moxey."

"That is very nice of you, Captain. I know they will all appreciate it."

"What you and the others did made a big difference to many people's lives."

"Well, you know how it is, Captain. We would expect others to do the same for us if we were in similar circumstances."

"I do wish you well, Mr. Bris-coe, in the event you decide not to return."

Briscoe paused to consider Leech's statement. He had been so busy lately, he hadn't given the idea of not returning much thought. "At this point, Captain, I don't expect I won't."

"Let's hope that is the case, but one never knows. You may think differently once you're home. In any event, it's been a great pleasure sailing with you."

Briscoe was taken aback. He had never heard Captain Tyler Leech say that to anyone. Briscoe knew the bond he and Leech shared was strictly a respect for each other's professionalism. However, there was the other common bond they shared: both men had lost their families. Leech understood what he must be or would be going through.

"You, too, Captain. Thank you."

They shook hands and parted.

■ ■ ■

With suitcase in hand, Briscoe and the Japanese agent walked the main deck toward the gangway. Along the way they passed Bosun Knuckles.

"Good job this tour, as always, Billy." Briscoe stopped and they shook hands.

"Thanks, Mr. Briscoe," Knuckles said. "You have a good vacation."

He passed other crewmembers on his way to the gangway. They wished him a safe trip home and a happy holiday season. Even though it was presently only two days after Labor Day, all hands knew his four-month vacation wouldn't put him back on the ship until sometime after the first of the year. They envied this lucky man who would be home for the holidays. Briscoe wished them all the same holiday greetings in return and bid them many safe voyages.

When he reached the gangway, he found a smiling Greta Moxey waiting there. She was on gangway watch. He put down his suitcase and gave her a hug. The Japanese agent waited impatiently with his hand on the gangway railing.

"I'm going to miss you, Miss Moxey," he said.

She hugged him back and said, "You, too."

"Thank you for your help. You did some remarkable things."

"Thanks," she said with appreciation. "It has been an interesting time, Mate. You have a nice vacation."

He nodded, picked up his suitcase, and started up the gangway. But then he stopped, turned around, and quickly walked back to her. He set his suitcase down on the deck and, to her surprise, he hugged her again.

157

"Lady, I must tell you, I've had a crush on you since the night you came sweeping into the CCR with your lovely, long hair, dressed to kill, and bearing gifts."

"Bearing gifts? Oh, you mean those silly chips?" she asked.

Briscoe nodded. "You'll have to remember in the future to be more cautious about giving potato chips to chief mates. They have an odd effect on a few."

Moxey laughed. "I'll try to remember that."

"Greta...there is no one else onboard this ship who cares more about you than I do."

Moxey smiled. Almost embarrassed, she said, "Okay, Mate. You can give me a break from the soft stuff now."

"Articulation of the heart has never been a strong suit of mine. What usually does filter out of my mouth represents only a small tip of a huge iceberg."

The Japanese agent stood on the gangway, impatiently looking at his watch and tapping his fingernails on the railing.

"That's sweet," she said.

"I wish it could be different, Greta."

"Me, too. Now, go home to your wife. She's waiting."

"Please be safe."

"I always am," she said with assurance.

They looked into each other's eyes and smiled.

At the nervous urging of the high-strung, Japanese agent who was in a hurry to get the chief mate to his scheduled flight on time, Briscoe left Greta Moxey and the *Majestic Prince* behind for home.

As Moxey watched him go, Hillert hollered down to her from the catwalk.

"Hey, Greta! The CCR is trying to call you on your radio."

"Oh?" She raised the radio to her mouth and spoke. "CCR, this is the gangway. Over."

There was no reply. She looked up at Hillert.

Hillert hollered down to her, "I can't hear you. Your radio's not working."

"Battery must be dead," she said.

She left the gangway and headed for the CCR where the batteries were kept.

■ ■ ■

Moxey entered the control room. Hubbard and Bensinger were talking.

"Excuse me, Mate," she said. "I think my battery is dead. Did you call me?"

Hubbard looked at her and said, "Yes, I did. I need the sailing board posted for 0800 tomorrow, please." Hubbard reached for the battery charger and pulled out a spare. "Here's a charged one."

"Thank you," she said as she took it.

"You're welcome," the chief mate said.

Moxey removed the back of her radio to change out the batteries while Hubbard and Bensinger continued to talk.

"So how's he doing, really?" Hubbard asked Bensinger.

"He's changed a lot, Barney. He's not the same. I've never seen him more withdrawn. It's like his spirit has been striped away."

Hubbard sighed. "Poor guy. Could he still do his job?"

Moxey swapped out batteries, but couldn't help but overhear the conversation. She wondered who they were talking about.

Bensinger answered, "Oh, yeah. No problem there. I mean, Jimmy's a professional, always. Hell, he, Dirk, and the others went over to this sinking ship in horrendous swells and saved some guy trapped under a beam. He was incredible. He never faltered once during any of it. I mean, he was *solid*." Bensinger then looked at Moxey at that point and asked, "Isn't that right, Greta?"

"What's that?" she asked, looking up from her radio.

"During the rescue, Chief Mate Jimmy never once showed any sign of weakness, did he?"

"No. Never," she answered, somewhat puzzled.

Hubbard shook his head. "It's amazing. I don't think I could have ever functioned if it were me. Poor guy."

Moxey was confused. She asked, "Excuse me, but who are you two talking about? Did something happen to Jimmy?"

Hubbard looked at Moxey, and then at Bensinger.

With incredulity, Bensinger asked, "He didn't tell you?"

"No. Tell me what?" Moxey asked.

"Oh, gosh. You don't know," Bensinger said with surprise. "Jimmy lost his family in a car crash eight months ago."

159

Moxey was stunned. Her mouth was open, but she was speechless. She looked at Hubbard for affirmation.

The chief mate nodded that it was true.

"I'm sorry," Bensinger apologized. "I knew he wanted it kept quiet, but I thought he had at least told you."

Hubbard added, "I thought everybody knew."

Moxey shook her head. "Oh, my..." was all she could say.

■ ■ ■

It was overcast when the taxi pulled up in front of the Vermont house. James Briscoe emerged with his suitcase. Kelley and Marta, the next-door neighbors, were in their front yard raking. Otto the sheepdog was with them. They exchanged warm greetings and when Otto saw his master, he ran to him. The big dog jumped on him and licked his face. Briscoe laughed and gave the dog a big hug. It then began to rain.

Briscoe went upstairs to hang up his clothes. He looked in Gilly's room. It was untouched. Toys littered the floor where his son had last played with them. He continued on and stopped in the doorway at Katey's room. He found it the same way.

A voice inside his head said, *Katey froze to death.*

He closed his eyes and rested his head on the doorway for a moment.

"Stop it!" he pleaded with himself.

He left Katey's doorway and wandered into his bedroom. Greta Moxey's words came to him.

If you don't make yourself happy, who else will?

He opened his suitcase and began removing his travel clothes. He then stepped into the walk-in, cedar closet to hang up his clean clothes. Upon entering, he saw all of Heather's clothes. Sam Waerhauser's words went through his mind as he hung up his shirt.

Heather would probably have wanted you to go out and have some fun instead of sit around and mope all day.

He sat down on the chair in the closet and rested his head in his hands. The rain continued to fall.

Chapter Thirteen

Leaving the Ashes Behind

It was a bright and sunny, spring day when the telephone rang in the den. Briscoe hurried to his desk. He was sweating from exercising as he answered the phone.

"Hello."

A familiar voice asked, "If you were the sun, what time would you set?"

Briscoe smiled. "Greta! Hi! How are you?"

Greta answered, "Hi, Mate. I'm good. I just got home a couple of days ago."

"I figured you'd be on vacation by now," he said. "How was your last trip?"

"Don't ask. It was terrible! I had four, dreadful months on the *Perseverance*. The captain over there treats his crew like dirt. It was nothing but four months of stress. I'm never going back to that ship again."

"Sorry to hear that. I just got back myself. I worked another four-month tour on the *Prince* again.

"Was it a good tour?"

"It was helpful. I needed to get out of the house bad."

Tenderly, Greta asked, "How are *you* doing, Mate?"

He knew she meant, "How are you dealing with your tragedy?"

Briscoe glanced around the den of his quiet house. "I'm fine, Greta. I, ah, just got your card." He picked up the card sitting on his desk. "Greta, I was going to tell you about my family, but it wasn't a good time for me. I'm sorry you found out from other people."

"I wish you had told me," she said.

"I didn't want anyone to know. I didn't want sympathy or advice from everyone. It's something *I* had to deal with. I still do."

"I can understand that," she said. "I just feel like such a jerk for making those references to your wife and all. I..."

"You didn't know. That's okay. Don't worry about it. Listen...thanks for the card. I appreciated it."

"Mate...the reason I'm calling is...I was wondering if I could see you?"

There was an eternal moment of silence. Greta sensed a rejection in the air.

Briscoe was unsure how to answer.

Life goes on, Briscoe! he said to himself. *Do something about it, idiot!*

Finally, he spoke. "I'd like that."

"Great!" Greta said, pleased. "Come down and visit me then."

■ ■ ■

The next day Briscoe left the house and Otto in the care of his next-door neighbors and drove to Greta's parents' home in Annapolis, eight hours away. Once in town he had little trouble following her directions and quickly found the Moxey's small ranch house in the suburbs. The springtime flowers were in bloom. Briscoe drove slowly through a neighborhood, spotted the house, and parked in front of it.

He knocked and Greta answered the door.

"Hi, Chief Mate," she said with delight and then gave him a hug.

"Hi, Greta," he said, happy to see her. He hadn't seen her in almost eight months and she hadn't changed. Her face had its usual radiant glow, her thick, rusty red hair was still long, and her figure still as shapely as ever.

"Let me look," she said gently pushing him away. "You haven't changed a bit."

"Neither have you."

"Where are you bags?"

"In the car. Why?"

"Let's get them. My folks want you to stay here."

Briscoe hadn't expected this. "I can't do that, Greta."

"Sure you can. They said it was all right. It was their idea."

"That's nice of them, but I don't want to impose on anyone. Just give me the name of a good motel nearby and-"

"Who's looking for a motel?" asked a deep, booming voice.

A large man in his early fifties dressed in a t-shirt and blue jeans suddenly appeared behind her.

"Daddy, this is Jimmy Briscoe. Jimmy, this is my dad."

Tom Moxey was a burly, solid-looking man. Six-foot-two, 220 pounds; complete with the beginnings of a middle age paunch. In his youth he might have been a formidable opponent on the wrestling mat. He stood there in the doorway holding a can of Moosehead beer in his left hand, sizing up his daughter's newest beau.

"Nice to meet you, Mr. Moxey," Briscoe said extending his hand.

"So this is the hero chief mate," Tom Moxey said, taking his hand and shaking it.

"Hero?" Briscoe asked, puzzled.

"I told Daddy about the baby delivery," Greta said.

"Oh, yes. Well, Mr. Moxey, you're daughter deserves equal credit for that. I couldn't have done it without her."

"Call me Tom. People calling me 'mister' make me feel like an old fart. Greta does a good enough job of that every time she comes home. What with all of her exercising and running around. It's enough to make my head spin."

He turned and called down the hallway. "Darlene...our visitor is here."

A moment later a large, buxom woman appeared in the hallway. She was wearing a sweat suit with an apron on over it. Apparently, she had been busy in the kitchen. She was a pretty lady, taller than Greta but shorter than Tom Moxey, with deep, red hair like Greta's.

"This is my mom," Greta said.

"I could tell. Hi, Mrs. Moxey."

"Call her Darlene," Tom interjected.

"Hello, Jimmy," she said warmly, taking his hand and squeezing it. "It's so nice to meet you. I've heard a great deal about you. What are you doing standing out there? Come on in."

"He's talking about finding a motel," Tom said, pretending to complain. "He hasn't been here more than two minutes and already the seaman in him is coming out."

"Daddy!"

163

Briscoe smiled. He liked Tom Moxey already.

"Just kidding, Little Red. A little, old Navy humor."

"A motel? What on earth for?" Mrs. Moxey asked, astounded.

"I don't want to impose, Mrs. Moxey," Briscoe said.

"Call her Darlene," Tom Moxey repeated.

"Nonsense! We have plenty of room. The other two kids are married and gone. The house is practically empty except when Greta comes home."

"My daughter says you're a nice guy. If that's true then you're not imposing," Tom Moxey added.

"Yes, and we would be badly hurt if you traveled all this way from Maine-"

"Vermont," Greta corrected.

"- from Vermont or wherever and decided to stay at a motel," Mrs. Moxey said.

"Well, if you insist-," Briscoe said glancing at Greta.

Greta stood there leaning against the doorway, smiling, as her parents smothered him with their brand of hospitality. She said, "It's useless, Chief Mate. You can't refuse. Let me help you with your bags."

Briscoe gave in and followed Greta to his car.

"They're nice people," he said. "It's good to see you again. You look wonderful."

"Thank you," Greta smiled. "So do you. I'm glad you're here. I can't wait to show you around."

The days in Annapolis were wonderful. Greta's parents were warm and gracious hosts. Tom Moxey was a hard-working, blue-collar type; a former Navy enlisted man. He was now a foreman at a local cannery. He was friendly and relaxed. He and Briscoe shared many a tall sea stories. Darlene Moxey was a grade school teacher. She was cheerful, thoughtful, and composed; a mother who'd do anything for her kids and grandkids. Between the two of them there was a true sense of love and family bonding. A typical American family. Briscoe liked that.

Greta and Briscoe went out to dinner and danced almost nightly. On one night, they stayed in and made dinner for her parents. On another night they took Tom and Darlene down to Ocean City and danced all night.

They went on a sightseeing trip up and down the eastern shore and they picnicked overlooking the bay. They were sitting on the ground on a picnic blanket enjoying lunch when Briscoe suddenly saw a ship coming up the bay.

He stood up and exclaimed, "Oh, no! Let's get out of here. Quick!"

"Why? What's the matter, Jimmy?"

"Look at that!"

"What? The *ship*?"

"Yeah. I'm getting a baaad headache.

She laughed. "Don't you just hate ships?"

"No...but I feel better when they're not around."

She then stood up and shouted to the world, "I love being on vacation!" She then said to him, "This day is so grand! So beautiful. Don't you just wish it would last forever?" She leaned forward and kissed him.

Briscoe was hesitant. He looked out at the bay. "Yes, I do. But...I've got to get back. Otto's probably driving my next door neighbors crazy."

"I'd like to meet this 'Otto' character some time."

Briscoe paused for a moment. After two, fun-filled weeks of being together, he decided to take a big step. He said, "You can. Would you like to come with me back to Vermont?"

She looked at him for a moment, and then she kissed him.

"Yes. I would."

■ ■ ■

The weather continued to be warm, rain-free, and clear for the daylong drive north to the Green State. The sunroof was open and the cool breeze blew in as they followed I-95 to the north. They joined I-87 in New Jersey, traveled northward, and eventually skirted the eastern side of the Adirondacks. They crossed Lake Champlain on the ferry.

They passed the Pristine Hills road sign and a short time later they were descending the steep, Briscoe residence driveway. Climbing out of the car, they could hear Otto barking from behind one of the large windows.

165

"Time to let out the beast," Briscoe said.

"I'm ready. Who's been feeding him?"

"My next door neighbors."

He walked to the front door, unlocked it, and opened one of the double doors. Otto charged out of the house to greet him, like Dino the pet dinosaur in the *Flintstones.* He barked excitedly and then pawed and climbed up on Briscoe, expecting a hug.

"Okay, boy. Take it easy."

Briscoe hugged his dog and gave him a noogie on the head with his knuckles.

Otto then spotted Greta and forgot all about his master. The dog bolted towards her like a charging steam locomotive, but instantly hit the brakes and stopped upon reaching her. He gave Greta the quick sniff test that dogs do and then climbed up on her, placing his paws on her shoulders.

"Otto! Get down!" Briscoe ordered.

"It's okay. I'm used to big dogs. So, you're the notorious Otto, huh?" Greta asked as she petted the big, furry animal and hugged him.

His curiosity satisfied, Otto then returned to Briscoe and followed him as he walked back to the car for the suitcases.

Taking a moment to admire the house, Greta said, "It's beautiful, Jimmy."

"Thank you," he said with pride as he took her suitcase out of the trunk. "Come on. I'll give you the grand tour."

He showed her the living room with its fireplace and sweeping, wide panes of glass, complete with a striking view of the Green Mountains and forests. He led her through the family room and into the kitchen.

Greta was astounded at the beauty. The huge windows throughout the first floor brought the magnificent green outdoors inside.

"Absolutely beautiful."

"I'll show you the upstairs," he said. Leading her to the second floor, he took their suitcases with him.

At the top of the stairs he said, "This is the guest room. Over here are the kids' rooms."

She noted that toys were littered on the floors of the two rooms as though the children had been playing with them only moments before. The patina of dust that covered them, however, told her that Briscoe had left them that way.

He added uneasily, "Forgive the mess. It's been this way since...well, you know. One of these days I'll get around to picking them up."

She smiled sympathetically. "They're cute rooms," she said.

"Yes, there are."

They continued through the hallway.

"This is the master bedroom," he said as he placed their suitcases on the floor. "In there is the bathroom and Jacuzzi."

Greta looked in and saw a large triangular window over the Jacuzzi. Again, nature was allowed inside the house. Through the glass was another breath-taking view of the mountains and forests.

"Wow. Nice," she complimented.

"Finally," he said, "here's the walk-in, cedar closet."

He opened the door for her to have a peek. Heather's clothes filled most of the dowel rods.

A disconcerting feeling passed through Greta when she looked; a feeling that Heather Briscoe was still very much alive and living in the house. She half-expected Heather to suddenly appear and introduce herself.

"And that's the tour."

"I'll say it again, Jimmy. It's a beautiful home."

"Thank you, Greta. Well, after that long drive I could use a drink. How about you?"

"I was about to ask for one," she said.

While Briscoe made daiquiris in the blender, Greta strolled through the kitchen and into the adjacent family room. There were more kids' toys in the corner. The end tables were graced with a few women's magazines. In another corner of the room a child's easel held a nearly completed work of finger-paint art. Even a quilt Heather had begun to sew still lay draped over one of the wing chairs. Everything seemed to be as it might have been before. Untouched.

She looked at the family photos that adorned the bookcases. The smiling children, the happy dog, the beautiful wife, and the handsome husband gave no evidence of a shattered home. The house still had the warm feeling of being inhabited by a loving family and that its members were merely away for the day. Greta's feeling of discomfort began to grow and she wondered how the visit would go, or even if she should stay long. She had the awful feeling she was walking around in a mausoleum or, better yet, a cenotaph. She tried to push those, what she knew were cruel, insensitive thoughts away. From the photos that were proudly sprinkled throughout the house, from the toys that embodied fantasy, playtime, and innocence, she could tell that at one time it had been a happy place - and still could be again.

"Here you are, Greta," Briscoe said, bringing in the drinks and handing her one.

"Thank you."

"Welcome to Vermont. Tomorrow I'll show you the sights."

They clinked their glasses.

"I'm glad you came," he said.

"I'm glad I came, too, Jimmy. Thank you for inviting me."

■ ■ ■

The spring sun set and night gradually came to Vermont. The brilliant green forests and the mountains slowly darkened and faded from view, causing the house windows to go black.

The day had been a long one and the tired couple prepared to go to bed.

Greta was in the bathroom, fresh from a clean, warm shower. Dressed in a pink nightie, she was brushing her long, rusty red hair in front of the mirror. She was preparing for him.

When she emerged she had more or less expected to find him lying in bed. Instead, she found him sitting on the side of the bed with only his shirt off. He was staring down at the floor.

He looked up at her and smiled, but it was a weak smile. Behind it she saw a withdrawn look in his face; the look of guilt which she had seen before.

"Jimmy, what's wrong?" she asked tenderly.

"I'm just thinking, that's all. Nothing's wrong. Everything's perfect. You're perfect. You look lovely," he assured her.

"Thank you," she said.

She understood his uneasiness. She was a little uneasy herself. He had shared that bed with only Heather for ten years. She looked briefly at Heather's bed; at Heather's things.

"Jimmy, it's all right with me if you prefer I spend the night in the guest room."

"No, don't be silly. It's okay. It's...it's new, that's all. I'll be all right. Come here," he said, marveling over her beautiful, red hair.

When she stood before him, he wrapped his arms around her and pulled her tight. She lightly followed the outline of his lips with her index finger. He then leaned back on the bed, bringing her gently down on top of him. They hugged and kissed. It was their first time ever and their passion for one another heated. Their arms squeezed each other tight. Their lips frantically searched out each other's mouths.

Suddenly, Briscoe stopped and stared at the ceiling.

"What's the matter, Jimmy?" she asked softly.

He looked at her, but didn't answer.

A short time later they found themselves in the guest room making love. The bed in the master bedroom was not turned down.

■ ■ ■

The next several days were happy ones, just like their days in Annapolis. They went boating and swimming in Lake Champlain. They rode the ferry and visited the islands. They took Otto and camped in the Green Mountain National Forest. They visited the Moss Glen Falls. They took in the Burlington nightlife and wined, dined, and danced. After a week, Greta no longer felt like a stranger in a house filled with ghosts. One week turned into two. The vacation went on and they laughed and they played. Spring became summer.

One warm and pleasant, summer night they lay on the grass in the backyard beneath the stars.

Briscoe looked up at the stars and said, "Do you know what this reminds me of?"

"What?"

"That night in Borneo when we rode the launch back to the ship."

"Our 'date' night," she said, and laughed. "You were a terrible dancer."

"I tried," he said, shrugging.

Briscoe smiled and gazed into her eyes.

"Greta, why didn't you call or write?" he asked.

"I knew you were in pain and needed to be alone. Anybody would in that situation. I didn't want to appear like an ambulance chaser," she said.

He nodded.

Greta saw sadness cross his face as he gazed skyward.

"You truly loved her, didn't you?"

His eyes drifted to the ground and he nodded again.

"Yes. She was a fine woman. A good friend. And she was so good with the kids. I should have quit shipping years ago. If I had, things might have been different today. I wouldn't have been going to the airport that day. They might still be here."

"Perhaps they would be," she said gently. "But you can't blame yourself, Jimmy. A lot of people go away to support their families. It's what they have to do. A lot of people stay ashore and go to work every day, too, and terrible things happen to them as well. The newspapers are full of horrible stories every day about things that happen to decent people."

"I don't know, Greta."

"The car accident...well, it was just that: a terrible, unfortunate accident. You're lucky you survived."

"I know," he sighed, caressing her knee. "It'll take time, Greta. You've been wonderful to me these last few weeks. I've been very happy. This house, this land, these trees, and Otto are all part of my past now and yet I don't want to ever let any of it go. This is all I have left to remind me of them. I don't want to let the memories ever fade away."

"You shouldn't forget them, Jimmy."

"My only regret is I never took the time to tell her how much I loved her and how wonderful this home was she had created for us."

"I think she'll know, somehow, Jimmy."

Briscoe looked at her, squeezed her hand, and smiled.

"You're a good woman, too, Greta."

"Thank you, Mate," she said cheerfully.

Briscoe studied her hand for a long moment and then her gray eyes.

"Greta...what would you say if I...were to ask you to marry me?"

She was taken aback. "I'd say 'thank you very much, but no thank you.' I'm not Heather."

"I know you're not. I'm not looking for someone to fill her shoes," he said.

"Do you remember that advice you gave me on the launch about getting involved with a man with marital problems? You said they should 'be avoided at all costs.' It sounded like wise advice at the time."

Briscoe nodded. "Greta, I know I have a lot of personal baggage that I'd be bringing along with me and it's going to take time. But I wouldn't expect you to be Heather. I love you because you are you. I'm ready to start over again."

She paused and then said, "I wouldn't tolerate cheating."

Briscoe was puzzled. "I never cheated. Besides, if we're together at home *and* at sea, how would I ever have a chance to fool around?"

"A seagoing couple?" she laughed. "On the *same* ship?"

"Sure, why not?"

"Me sailing as AB and you the chief mate? My boss?"

"Yes!"

"The rest of the crew would hate me! They'd say you were giving me more overtime. They'd say I was a direct pipeline to you and that I'd be telling you who was slacking off."

"So, let them! I don't care! And if one of us decides we've had enough of going to sea, we'll *both* quit."

Greta smiled, disbelieving. "Those are the terms? You'll quit if I do?"

"Yes."

"Promise?"

"Promise. I left one love long enough. I don't want to leave another."

"Okay, James Briscoe, 'best chief mate this side of the date line.' You've got yourself a deal."

They kissed and rolled on the ground.

Chapter Fourteen

And Then There was Greta Moxey

Briscoe and Greta flew back to work together in September and joined the *Majestic Prince* in Osaka.

While at home in the states they had set a tentative wedding date for the second weekend in January. Greta's parents were thrilled when they heard the news and offered to begin making arrangements while the couple was at sea.

Needless to say, Greta was surprised two days after leaving Japan when she found an invitation slipped under her door. It was to her *own* wedding - on the ship of all places! On Halloween of all days!

She ran up the two decks to Briscoe's office.

"This is crazy!" she said happily, waving the invitation back and forth in the air.

"Isn't it?" he said with glee.

"This is so unique!" she said excitedly. "What about Mom and Dad? They'd be so disappointed to miss the wedding."

"We'll still have the ceremony in January when we return to the states."

Greta paused to think.

"Well?" he asked, impatiently.

"'Well,' what?" she asked, joyfully mocking his impatience.

"Do you accept the invitation?"

"How could I ever refuse the best chief mate on this side of the dateline?" Greta stepped forward to him and kissed him. "I love you, Jimmy."

■ ■ ■

On wedding day, chief cook Fritz Sonnenschmidt put the finishing touches on the cake. The cake was three-feet-tall and had five-levels.

Dirk Mainline, the first engineer, walked through the galley and saw it. "It's a beautiful cake, Fritz," praised the first engineer.

Fritz agreed whole-heartedly. "Yes, yes. Absolutely. It is a beautiful cake. Watch it! Don't lean too close. You might touch it with your dreadlocks."

Captain Leech was delighted with Briscoe's request and quickly agreed to perform a shipboard wedding. He was honored to be asked.

The couple planned to honeymoon in Hawaii as soon as they were relieved in mid-December. They were going to stay there through Christmas. Returning home afterwards, they planned to have a regular wedding for the benefit of the family and friends; especially since a shipboard wedding performed by a captain and witnessed by the crew was really nothing more than a civil ceremony with the captain serving as "window dressing."

The wedding ceremony was held on the *Majestic Prince's* starboard bridge wing on Halloween. The ship was southbound in the South China Sea that day. It was not very far from the position where Typhoon Angela had parked herself and ravaged the sea a little more than a year ago. Unlike the tumultuous weather of that busy voyage, it was a clear, sunny day and the sea was calm. The seasonal monsoonal winds were light, the northeasterly winds were behind the *Prince,* and there was little air movement across the deck.

Most of the off-duty crewmembers surrounded the couple while a few scurried around snapping pictures of the big event - the first and only one of its kind in GascoTrans history. Below in the galley, extensive preparations were being made for the reception on the pool deck. Steward Stancy wanted to create a feast that would never be forgotten.

Greta stood magnificently in her wedding gown; the world's most beautiful bride. The gown had come from a fashionable shop in Osaka. Fritz and Greta had gone off three weeks earlier to order it. Fortunately, it had arrived in time during the last trip.

Briscoe was dressed smartly in a gray suit he had brought from home.

Captain Leech was dressed up in his old, Navy whites. Briscoe had no idea why the Old Man had his whites on board to begin with since they weren't part of the company uniform, but he was glad he had them. He thought the Old Man looked quite snazzy standing there in his sterling outfit. It lent more of an official air to the ceremony.

As he stood there gazing at his new bride and listening to Leech read on about holy matrimony, pangs of his past began to sting at him. He heard voices from within.

Heather.

The kids.

He tried to put the thoughts, the *voices,* out of his head, but they persisted.

Heather. Katey. Gilly.

Don't feel guilty. She would have wanted it this way.

It wasn't your fault they died.

Katey. Gilly. Heather.

Katey froze to death.

Katey froze *to death!*

Briscoe glanced beyond Captain Leech at his friend Sam. Sam returned his glance. Sam nodded and smiled. He heard Sam's voice from the past. *She would have wanted it this way. Don't feel guilty. She would have wanted you to be happy. That's all Heather ever wanted for you, Jimmy. Your happiness. Remember that. Remember what you learned the first time around.*

Briscoe looked at Greta.

Gilly. Heather. Katey.

Remember the mistakes. Don't let them happen with Greta. <u>*Don't let them happen with Greta!*</u> the voice repeated.

"I won't," Briscoe answered.

"What?" Greta whispered.

"Nothing," he said with assurance and smiled. "Nothing."

When Captain Leech had finished reading, he put his book down and looked at Briscoe. He nodded and said, "Jimmy."

That was Briscoe's cue. Prior to the wedding ceremony, both he and Greta had agreed to "customize" it a bit, with each of them saying something to each other they felt was meaningful to themselves and to their vows.

With the crew watching, Briscoe took her hands into his and held them gently. He then looked into his lovely bride's awaiting, bright, gray eyes and said, "First there was the sky...the clouds...and the blue ocean. And then there was Greta Moxey.

And Heather
I do take you to be my wife. Forever."

He then placed a ring on her finger.

Greta beamed an enormous smile. It was the first time she had ever heard those lovely words in her life and she was touched. Her heart soared.

Captain Leech then looked at her and said, "Your turn, Greta."

Greta had some trouble opening her mouth at first for she was choked up after hearing Briscoe's sweet words. She had never been in so much love before in her life. She was unaware that people could love one another as much as she was in love with Jimmy Briscoe at that very moment.

A few seconds passed. She finally gained control of herself and spoke to her patiently waiting bridegroom.

She said, "I do take you, Jimmy Briscoe, the best chief mate on this side of the dateline, to be my mate. Forever." Likewise, she placed a ring on his finger.

There was mild, approving laughter amongst the crew over Greta's play on words. When the laughter had faded, Captain Leech spoke.

"With the limited power invested in me as master of this vessel, I now pronounce you man and wife. You may now kiss the bride."

Briscoe and Greta became locked in embrace and kissed for what seemed like an eternity. The crew gathered around them and showered them with the rice that Steward Stancy had brought up from the galley. There were cheers and laughter and many pats on the back and congratulations and handshakes. The kiss went on and on, however, and, one by one, the crewmembers ran out of rice to toss and became bored with the newlyweds. Like most seaman in search of a good time, they went off to the reception down on the pool deck, leaving the newlyweds by themselves on the bridge wing.

■ ■ ■

Stancy and Fritz had outdone themselves. The wedding reception was first-rate. The pool deck was lined with tables on which a cuisine fit for royalty was served. In the middle of the main center table stood the grand, three-foot-tall, five-level cake that Fritz had spent the entire previous day baking.

There was even dance music, provided by the efforts of a makeshift band composed of a few crewmembers that had brought their instruments.

During the reception Greta handed Briscoe a small, gift-wrapped box.

"Here's your wedding present, Jimmy," she said.

He unwrapped the cheerfully wrapped box. Inside, he found a pair of red and green, cotton work gloves.

"Thanks, Greta," he said with a laugh. "I have something for you, too."

He removed a little box from his suit coat pocket and handed it to her. Greta opened it and found a gold, heart-shaped locket on a chain.

"Oh, how pretty," she said. She then opened the locket and let out a big laugh.

"Just what I wanted: a picture of Otto. Thank you, Jimmy."

Greta kissed and hugged him.

When their lips parted Briscoe said, "If you were the sun, I'd hope you never set."

As the festivities being held in their honor went on, the couple slipped quietly away and went to the 04 deck. Just outside his office door Briscoe swept his new bride off her feet and was about to carry her across the threshold.

"Is this consummation going to be on overtime?" she asked playfully.

"No way," he said, adamantly shaking his head.

"No way? Why not?" she demanded.

"It's not in your union contract."

"What a minute!" Greta said, kicking her legs in mild protest. "I want to call a union meeting first!"

"Later," Briscoe said. He carried her into his room and kicked the door shut.

The *Majestic Prince* continued to sail southbound in the South China Sea as the party went on, without them, late into the night.

■ ■ ■

Life for a couple aboard ship was wonderful.

Being married to Greta Moxey and having her on the ship was pure heaven. Briscoe had never been happier or less lonely in all of his life. He knew he'd never be alone again. He continued to have bouts with his guilt feelings over Heather and the children. He knew he always would. He missed them all terribly. At least Greta Moxey was there with him, a part of him now, and that would make him happy and help to relieve the pain he knew he would be carrying for a long, long time to come.

The shortened, three-month tour went fast. Before they knew it, they were preparing for their trip home. They had planned a two-week honeymoon stopover in Maui on their way back to the states. They had made their hotel reservations over the phone during the *Prince's* discharges in Japan. The airline reservations were being handled by the company since it was their responsibility to transport its crew personnel.

A week before they were to disembark the *Prince* in Japan, Briscoe and Greta were in Briscoe's office looking over literature on Maui when Captain Leech entered with a telex in his hand.

"Mr. and Mrs. Bris-coe, your flight arrangements just came in from the agent. Here...you take the white copy and I'll keep the yellow and blue copies. This silly company wants records of every shred of paper that comes aboard the ship," Leech complained.

"Wonderful, Captain. Thank you," Briscoe said as he took the telex and glanced over its contents. "This is perfect. We got the flight we requested, Greta. Flight 573, Osaka to Honolulu."

"Oh, that's great! Maui here we come. I can't believe we're going. I've always wanted to see Hawaii," she said, and hugged Leech happily. "Thank you, Captain."

Captain Leech seemed a trifle uncomfortable over the display of affection. He had the feeling he was intruding.

"As you know, Mr. Bris-coe, it has always been my policy that there shall be no fraternizing with the crew. However, you and your new bride here have forced me to modify my position on the subject."

Briscoe smiled to himself as he saw Leech softening. It was funny watching the Old Man melt in Greta's presence.

"Good thing, too, Captain," Greta said putting her hand on his shoulder. "Otherwise, I'd be awfully mad if I couldn't speak to my own husband for four months."

"In your case, Greta, I must say that I whole-heartedly find you a delight and have no trouble fraternizing with you."

■ ■ ■

The next day the ship docked at the Osaka Terminal and Greta's relief came aboard and assumed her duties. Greta was now free to go on vacation with her new husband. Leaving her suitcases at the gangway, Greta entered the control room and found Briscoe, Bensinger, and Japanese representatives busy making preparations for discharging the cryogenic cargo. She was nicely dressed for shore and had a carry bag slung over her shoulder. She wore Jimmy's gold locket around her neck.

"I've got my relief, Mate. Where's yours?" she asked.

Briscoe was concerned. "Good question, Greta. Captain Leech is talking to the agent about it right now. He said he'd call me right back."

"About what?" she asked.

The telephone rang.

"Just a second. That's him." He answered the phone. "CCR, Chief Mate." There was a pause as he listened. "Yes, Captain."

She looked at Bensinger and asked, "What's going on?"

Before Brad could answer, she saw a look of disappointment sweep over her husband's face.

Briscoe said, "Okay, Captain. Thank you. Yes, I'm sorry, too." He hung up the phone.

"What's wrong?" Greta asked.

"Barney's not coming. His wife went into labor prematurely again and he didn't want to leave her. I have to make one more trip."

Unaffected, Greta said, "Well, no problem. I'll make one more trip, too."

Briscoe shook his head. "You can't. Your relief is already here. Leech says you have to get off."

"Oh," she said, disappointed.

"Damn. Some way to start off a honeymoon."

"Don't worry, Jimmy," Greta said trying to cheer him up. "It's only a two-week trip to Bontang. I'll wait for you in Hawaii. By the time you arrive, I'll have a nicer tan and look sexier than ever for you."

■ ■ ■

Briscoe walked Greta down to the gangway where the Japanese agent was waiting for her. He kissed his happy bride good-bye.

"You be safe and stay out of trouble," he said to her.

She snapped to attention and saluted him. "Yes, sir, Chief Mate."

Greta then started down the gangway, her long, thick, rusty red hair trailing behind her. The Japanese agent carrying her suitcase huffed and puffed to keep up with her.

"I'll see you in Hawaii," he said.

"I'll be there keeping the daiquiris cold for us!"

Marriage hadn't changed her one bit, he thought. And nor would he let it. She was still the free spirit he had fallen in love with and he vowed to himself he would do what he had to do to preserve her that way.

Once on the dock, Greta turned and looked up at him. She beamed a radiant grin and waved enthusiastically. Briscoe waved back. She was happier than she had ever been in her life. She loved and was proud of her chief mate husband.

Briscoe said to himself, "That's one happy girl."

The huffing, puffing agent then led her to his car and a minute later they were gone. She was off and Hawaii was going to be another one of life's pleasant adventures for her. He stood by the gangway for a moment and watched them drive away. He was sad to see her go without him.

Briscoe felt a small pang of heartache as he watched the car carrying his new bride disappear down the road; a pang leftover from the earlier days; of the days and nights without Heather and the kids; the pang of loneliness. He caught himself before he had a chance to fall into a pit of self-pity and tossed those thoughts out of his mind. In two weeks he would be with her again and they would have the time of their lives; their long, awaited honeymoon. He knew it would be the best honeymoon any couple could ever dream of having.

He then smiled to himself and thought with self-deprecation, "Surely I can survive two, short weeks."

■ ■ ■

He returned to the CCR and continued monitoring the discharge operation. The discharge went uneventfully, except for a few brief moments when he received a Marisat call from Barney Hubbard.

Back in the United States, a partying, jubilant Hubbard had called to tell him Marilee had given birth to a healthy baby boy, and that both mother and child were doing great! The man had been celebrating so hard, he could barely speak. He slurred every word and giggled in-between. Briscoe figured Hubbard wouldn't remember making the expensive, eight-dollar per minute satellite call until the day his phone bill arrived.

Brad Bensinger, Mike Heyerdahl, and Paul Lindvall let out joyous yells of approval when Briscoe relayed the good news. The three Japanese interpreters who were stationed in the control room curiously looked on at the brief commotion. When informed of the news, they, too, let out a loud round of cheers for they all knew and liked chief mate Barney Hubbard.

At first light the next morning, the mooring wires were let go, and the ship sailed. Once clear of Tomagashima Suido, the *Majestic Prince's* course was set, once again, to the south for Borneo. The day was beautiful, Briscoe observed as he stood on the main deck looking out at the horizon. The sea was calm, the sun was bright, and the sky was blue. A perfect day for a flight to Hawaii, he thought.

First there was the sky, the clouds, and the blue ocean. And then there was Greta Moxey.

He smiled when he remembered saying those words to her at the wedding.

"Oh, yes," he said warmly to himself. "I'll survive two, short weeks." He then returned to his room.

Despite the sharp pangs of heartache that he knew would eventually dull and heal, Jimmy Briscoe glanced at the pair of red and green cotton, work gloves Greta had given him for a wedding gift. They sat on the corner of his desk. He then looked at the photo of he and Greta holding little Kinh Moxey-Briscoe Dien.

He was the happiest man in the world.

■ ■ ■

That night the *Majestic Prince* was one hundred and thirty-six miles off the Japanese coast, her bow slicing through the calm sea at a leisurely sixteen knots. The beautiful day had continued into the night and the sky overhead was nothing but a spectacular three hundred and sixty-degree sphere of stars.

It was a quiet night aboard the LNG carrier. Most of the crew was asleep that first night out to sea - as usual. They were always tired after squeezing as much partying as possible into the brief amount of shore time available. The 02 and 03 decks were silent.

The 04 deck was quiet as well. Both Captain Leech and Briscoe were in their own rooms at opposite ends of the deck listening to *Voice of America.* Leech was relaxing in his recliner. Briscoe sat at his desk working on the middle-of-the-month crew overtime sheets. The only sound heard on the 04 deck was the music from both their radios spilling faintly into the passageway. Bing Crosby was singing "Have Yourself a Merry Little Christmas."

"Mother Hen Briscoe can take a break," he said to himself.

He, like most chief mates, considered himself to be like a mother hen taking care of their flock. The flock always needed guidance, first aid, an ear to listen; someone to show them the way during moments of darkness and uncertainty. At sea, for many, there were always moments of darkness and uncertainty; when a calm head was called for; when someone who had the answer was required.

Jimmy Briscoe...the best chief mate this side of the dateline! he smiled, thinking of Greta's words at the wedding.

The best chief mate this side of the dateline, he reflected. *Now, maybe I will be.*

The overtime papers were piled high in standard, Briscoe-disorganized fashion as he continued to work. The Christmas carols ended and a news broadcast began. While the *Voice of America's* monotonic announcer talked on in the background, Briscoe paid little attention to the broadcast. He found himself suddenly immersed in ordinary seaman Darryl Hawkins' botched-up overtime sheet. Darryl was perpetually mixing up the dates and hours he worked. And his penmanship was atrocious. Using the bosun's work logbook in which he noted when a crewmember worked, Briscoe had to reconstruct Darryl's workday and award the proper number of hours accordingly. Darryl was now one heck of a good seaman, but his record keeping of his own overtime sheet was as reliable as Ronald Reagan's memory.

181

"If I can straighten him out on how to write up an overtime sheet, he'll be a one hundred percent, number one, ordinary seaman," Briscoe thought.

It was during this thought that Briscoe's ear caught the tail end of a *VOA* news story about a plane crash. He corrected another mistake on Darryl's sheet and listened a little more closely to the broadcast. The report of plane crashes always riveted one's attention and Briscoe was no different than anyone else.

"...the aircraft suddenly did a severe bank to the left and plummeted into the ocean just five miles short of the runway at Honolulu International Airport. Tower controllers had the aircraft in sight and several of those who had witnessed the accident from pleasure boats said an engine exploded, destroying flight 573's left wing..."

Briscoe looked up from his paperwork.

573?

"What was our flight?" his lips whispered to the air.

Briscoe began to dig through the mound of papers that cluttered his desk, looking for the flight telex Captain Leech had given he and Greta only days ago.

That was *our flight number. Wasn't it?*

No!

He dug slowly at first, but as a horrible realization began to flood his mind he dug faster and faster. He rose from his desk and shoved his chair away for more room to search the desk. Beads of sweat began to form on his forehead.

"...there were no survivors...," the *VOA* announcer continued.

No! No!

"Where is that damn telex with the flights??" he cursed angrily to himself, nearly on the verge of panic, as he fought through the clutter of paperwork on the desk.

A weak knock at his door interrupted the rising panic within him. He looked up and saw Captain Leech. Leech's haggard face was long and pale. It was pained and agonized. It was full of sympathy and sorrow.

Briscoe had never seen the captain look this way before.

"No."

They were even tears in Leech's eyes.

NO! NO!

In his hand Leech held a yellow copy of the flight telex.

Briscoe stopped his manic search and looked pleadingly at Leech, praying that his worst fears were totally wrong. He looked deep into the Old Man's watery eyes and before he asked the question he knew the horror of the inevitable answer. His own face went pale and his voice was weak and cracked as tears of his own swelled and spilled from inside.

"Is it the same flight?" Briscoe managed to say. It came out as a whisper.

Leech lowered his head and nodded.

"Oh, God! No!" Briscoe cried out in horror. "No, no! Greta!" He hit his fist on the desk. He looked helplessly out through the blackness of his porthole into the night and then sat down, put his head to his desk, and sobbed uncontrollably. "Oh, no, Greta. Heather. Greta. No...no...please no. Please no."

First there was the sky, the clouds, and the blue ocean. And then there was Greta Moxey.

A moment later there was another knock at his door. It was Sam. Sam looked at the distressing scene before him and was baffled. There was a long-faced Captain Leech standing in the doorway watching a sobbing Jimmy Briscoe.

"What's happened?" he asked.

"Greta was on an airliner that went down," Leech said.

"That's not so," Sam said, puzzled.

"We just heard it on the radio," Leech said.

"No, it's not so," Sam repeated. "Greta's on the Marisat right now and she wants to talk to you, Jimmy."

Briscoe was stunned. "What?"

Without waiting for an answer, he shot up out of his seat, ran passed both men, and raced down the passageway to the radio shack.

"Greta??" he said with desperation as he seized the Marisat phone off the desk.

"Jimmy!" Greta's voice said excitedly.

"Oh, thank God! You're alive!" he said with relief as he closed his eyes.

"I'm all right! I just heard the horrible news about our flight and I knew you'd be terrified."

"I was! Where are you?"

"I'm still in Japan. I missed the flight! The agent got hung up in rush hour traffic after leaving the ship and I wound up being delayed all the way to Narita."

"Thank God for that! Greta, I love you. I don't know what I would have done without you."

"I love you, too, Jimmy. I can't wait to be with you in Hawaii."

"Soon. Very soon, honey." Briscoe paused to catch his breath. He then said, "Greta, do you think you could get to Hawaii another way?"

"Like how?" she asked.

"Say, by ship?"

Greta laughed and said, "After three months of being stuck on one? No way, Chief Mate!"

Briscoe laughed, too. "Stop calling me 'Chief Mate,' will you?"

"I'll stop calling you Chief Mate as soon you're off the ship."

"I'll see you soon. I love you."

"I love you, too, Jimmy. I love you, too."

The light from the radio shack poured through the round porthole of the *Majestic Prince's* house as the huge, LNG carrier made her way silently through the sea toward a twilight horizon. As one ascends higher and higher above the surface into the clear night sky at great speed, the little, round light becomes nothing more than a white speck against a vast, black velvet background; a background whose only boundary is formed by the horizon line separating it from the sphere of stars above. It was all alone and insignificant, miniscule and defenseless.

A moment later the white speck disappeared.

ACKNOWLEDGEMENTS

I would like to thank these individuals and organizations for their support and contributions, and for those who took the time to read and comment on the finished work. I am truly grateful for their efforts.

Susan Dickens
Lindsey Dickens
Susanne Kennedy
Sara Yerkovich
Bob Anthony
Kathleen Moxey
Becky Northup
Bob Roes
Ike Isenstadt
Elaine Gotham of Gotham City Design (585-374-9585)
The Marine Engineers' Beneficial Association, Washington, DC
The South Bristol Cultural Center, Inc.,
    5323 Seneca Point Rd, Canandaigua, NY (585-396-5950)

Cover imagery courtesy of NOAA National Environmental Satellite Data and Information Service, NOAA National Geophysical Data Center, The Defense Meteorological Satellite Program F-13 2.7 km visible imagery, ETOPO2 2 Minute Global Elevations and the Van Sant Vegetation Index. Composition of Typhoon Bilis, August

21, 2000 at 0937Z, NOAA Environmental Visualization program. Many thanks also to Tim Loomis, NOAA EVP Media Lab Architect.

And finally, I wish to thank my shipmates during the nineteen year period that I had the privilege of being a deck officer aboard the M.E.B.A.-manned, American fleet of LNG carriers that, since 1977, were operated in the orient by Energy Transportation Corporation/ Pronav. I worked with a lot of fine professionals and learned a lot from so many; too many to name here. In the fall of 2000, after a lengthy legal battle and a disappointing defeat, the American flags on this respected fleet were taken down and replaced with the Marshall Islands flag. The 176 dedicated, American officers onboard were replaced with multinationals. I wish my former shipmates well in their new endeavors.

Larry Dickens, 5/22/02

About The Author

Larry Dickens holds an unlimited oceans master's license and is a freelance writer whose nonfiction work has appeared in several maritime publications. In 2000, he completed a twenty-four-year maritime career where he spent most of his seagoing time aboard LNG supertankers operating in the Orient. In addition to writing contemporary sea novels, he writes purposeful children's novels (*Mrs. McGillacuddy's Garden Party; Hillary's Wish*), as well as screenplays of his work. He resides in the Finger Lakes region of New York State with his wife, Susan, and two daughters.

Mr. Dickens welcomes your thoughts about this book and can be reached at SuLindHill@aol.com. Visit his website for future releases at www.larrydickens.com (or http://members.aol.com/sulindhill).

Printed in the United States
1059300001B/262-360